Also by Susan Dunlap

Karma
An Equal Opportunity Death
As a Favor
The Bohemian Connection
The Last Annual Slugfest
Not Exactly a Brahmin
Too Close to the Edge
Diamond in the Buff
A Dinner to Die For
Pious Deception
Rogue Wave
Death and Taxes
Time Expired

THE BOHEMIAN CONNECTION

A Mystery

SUSAN DUNLAP

A DELL BOOK

Published by
Dell Publishing
a division of
Bantam Doubleday Dell Publishing Group, Inc.
1540 Broadway
New York, New York 10036

ISBN: 0-440-21569-2

Printed in the United States of America

Published simultaneously in Canada

October 1994

10   9   8   7   6   5   4   3   2   1

RAD

For Marcia Muller

CHAPTER

1

"The reason I *am* raising my voice," I said, vainly trying to control it, "is that it's after noon; I've got sweat running down my arms, my back, my chest, and all over my face. I've spent the last two hours trying to get my truck off the edge of the hillside ten miles out of town so it, and I, wouldn't go careening down into a creek. There was no house for miles in either direction. If some guy with a pickup hadn't come along I'd still be there." I glared at my boss, Mr. Bobbs, the manager of the Henderson Pacific Gas and Electric office.

"I *am* submitting a request for repair of the truck, Miss Haskell. That is procedure." In contrast to my sweat-stained meter-reader uniform, Mr. Bobbs's tan summer suit was dry and crisp. And here in his windowless cubicle, the manager's office, it was almost cool, unlike the ninety-seven degrees outside.

I swallowed, using the time to control my anger. Slowly, I said, "This is hardly the first time a meter reader has been stuck on a back road. Suppose one of us were in an accident. He could be injured. It could be days before anyone discovered him."

Mr. Bobbs shifted his gaze to the clock behind me, silently stating that it was his lunch hour, too.

"There are a lot of dangerous people in those hills. They have guns. There are marijuana growers; the last thing they want is someone in a uniform coming onto their land. They've been known to shoot first and check out which department you work for after."

"Are you telling me you want to work only town routes?"

It was tempting after the morning's frustration. But I said, "No, I'm not asking to shift the danger to someone else. I'm saying I gave you a very reasonable suggestion for how to deal with this problem."

He nodded, a motion that did not mean he agreed with my suggestion, or even that he recalled what it was, but merely that he acknowledged that I said I had made one.

"I gave it to you a month ago."

He nodded again. The muscles around his mouth and neck tightened, leaving folds of skin hanging like a worn white scarf. "I put it in Follow-up," he said.

"Follow-up! You stuck my suggestion in a folder that won't come back to you till next week, or next month, or whatever date you put on it! By that time one of us could be lying dead on some back road."

"I've scheduled your request to return to my desk on a date when I have the proper amount of time to deal with it. Now," he said, taking an anxious breath, "it is well after twelve, and I have other responsibilities. I will call you in when the Follow-up folder with your suggestion comes back."

If you don't just plunk it in another Follow-up folder for an even later date, I wanted to add. But I didn't. Instead, I walked out of the cubicle and back to the storeroom in the rear of the office. My route book was still in the middle of the old wooden table, where I had dropped it before stalking into Mr. Bobbs's office. The tan duffle-like San Francisco bag that carried the completed route books to the computer in the city was waiting in the corner. And by the board where we hung the truck keys stood my fellow meter reader, Vida Riccolo.

"Are you okay, Vejay?" she asked.

"After a fashion. I told Mr. Bobbs—"

"I know what you told him. All of the Russian River Resort Area knows, or they would if his office had a window. Come on, what you need is a beer. I could use one myself." She looked like she needed a drink.

"Right." I stuck the route book in the San Francisco bag, relieved that there had been no "changes" (too great an electricity usage or suspiciously little) in any of the customers' reads that needed to be mentioned to Mr. Bobbs. I put the truck keys on the board and signed out.

Vida was parked outside the gate of the truck yard. With her short, thick curly hair and her deeply tanned skin she looked more like a little boy than a forty-five-year-old woman.

"So?" she prompted as I climbed into her pickup.

I shrugged. "My truck is a hazard. This time the reverse gear wouldn't work. You heard what I told Mr. Bobbs; you know how I spent the morning. But that's not really the issue. The thing is, anyone can get stuck back in the hills, and it's dangerous out there. There are Vietnam vets who've lived off the land since they got back who still can't deal with people. And there are our own homegrown drunks and crazies. It's wild country. And we need two-way radios in the trucks. I told Mr. Bobbs that a month ago."

"What did he say?"

"He put my suggestion in Follow-up."

"Never do today what you can put off till tomorrow, and tomorrow, and tomorrow." Her normally animated voice sounded flat. "Follow-up is the answer to a bureaucrat's prayers."

"In the meantime," I went on, "Mr. Bobbs said he had other responsibilities, by which I assume he meant lunch."

While I had been talking—complaining—we'd driven the commercial block of North Bank Road, inching through town in low gear. In summer, Henderson and the whole Russian River Resort Area was jammed with tourists. And now, the first weekend of Bohemian Week, traffic barely moved. The same people who in March sat in their San Francisco or Oakland living rooms watching television coverage of the Russian River flooding and asked each other how anyone could be crazy enough to live where the streets washed out and their homes filled with mud and debris every few years, now jammed the roads. They crowded onto the main beach in Guerneville and filled the little town beach here in Henderson. They stayed two, three, four to a room in ramshackle motels by the river, the same motels that had been three feet deep in water in March. Those old motels and "vacation cabins" were never quite clean and preserved the odor of mildew from year to year. But the families that came for a week of canoeing and swimming in the deep waters behind the summer dams didn't care. For them the river provided a cheap traditional family vacation. Most of the summer the Russian River area was peopled with a combination of tourist families and the newly insurgent gay population, who viewed the area as a haven of their own. Then there were the winter people like me, who, grumbling at the inconvenience, opened canoe rentals and summer shops, who double-stocked their shelves and made more money in those three months than in the rest of the year.

And in the ten days of July known as Bohemian Week, the Bohemian Grove hosted the business and political leaders of the nation. The area filled with their assistants and servants, with reporters and photographers, and, as with any convention, with pimps and prostitutes—another boon to motel owners and shopkeepers.

The Grove was reputed to be a glorified boys' camp where for ten days the rich and powerful could cavort with impunity, secure from the eyes of the uninvited. Bohemian Club members included the President of the United States, presidents of multinational corporations, and even the chairman of the board of PG&E, though not all members attended each encampment. They were reported to put on skits in drag, get drunk, and pee in the bushes. Like Boy Scouts, they lived in tents, albeit luxurious ones, and competed to see whose chef was best. During Bohemian Week, helicopters flying in caviar and Dom Perignon were not uncommon sights. And although there was supposed to be a ban on discussion of business, major speeches at encampments in the past had been given by men like Henry Kissinger and Caspar Weinberger. The Bohemian Club publication even stated that the idea for the Manhattan Project, which led to the atom bomb, came out of one Bohemian Week. While all that went on, the public was barred from the grounds, as was the press, and women in any capacity. The anti-woman rule was so strongly enforced that we women weren't even allowed to read their meters during those ten days.

When the limousines of the powerful arrived out-side the Grove they would be greeted by lines of protesters—anti-nuclear, anti-poverty, anti-military. But the people of Henderson viewed the encampment with amusement. Whatever the big shots did in private, they brought publicity to the area and plenty of money to the town.

And a lot of cars and people. The limos would start coming this evening. Our congressman would be in town Sunday. But already the advance people, the newspeople, and the hangers-on were here.

"Where are we going?" I asked as Vida started up the hill away from the main street. "I thought we were headed for a beer."

"We are—at my niece's house."

Her normally energetic voice was almost still. I realized that we had sat in silence since the end of my jeremiad. There were fatigue lines around her mouth, dark circles under her eyes.

"You look worn out, Vida. That's not like you. You can usually go twice as long as anyone else."

She turned left onto a narrow hillside street. "Michelle," she said in a barely audible voice. "My niece Michelle, she didn't come home last night. I don't know what happened to her."

I waited for Vida to go on.

"Craig, her husband, didn't call me till this morning. I guess he didn't want to worry me. He should have called last night. This morning I couldn't take time off from work. You know Michelle, don't you?"

It was like Vida to assume that I would. Vida had grown up in Henderson, raised three sons here, then finally, years after she should have, divorced their father and left him to the bottle. Anybody in town was either a relative, one of her husband's relations, a son's friend, someone from St. Agnes' Church, or at least someone she had met doing one of the town routes.

"I might know her by sight," I said. Having lived here only a year and a half, with no husband now, and no children, my acquaintances were more limited. From reading the town routes I knew most people in a general way. I knew about their electricity usage, I knew if they weeded their yards or fixed their porches, I knew about their dogs and cats, and I knew the odd tidbits people chose to tell me. But I didn't know the most basic things about many people—where, or if, they worked, how many children they had, how they voted, or what they liked to read. In spite of that, as Vida pulled up in front of a new chalet-type house, I realized that I did know her niece.

"I've read Michelle's meter here. She's very pretty, isn't she? She looks something like you, Vida, but her hair is long, darker, and curled back. And she has," I paused, hunting for the right words, "a lot of curiosity and drive."

"You don't need to be polite, Vejay. What you mean is that Michelle can be a pain in the behind."

"No, I don't. Well, not after you know her. At first, when she stopped me to complain about her bill, I would have agreed with you. According to her then, not only was I incompetent, but PG and E was corrupt and focused entirely on cheating her and those like her."

Vida nodded knowingly.

"But Vida, once I showed her how to read her meter, and gave her the tips on saving electricity, then she was really enthusiastic. The next month she was waiting for me by the meter with her figures ready, anxious to see if she had read it right." I smiled. "She was pretty proud of how much energy she saved. She had reason to be."

Vida pulled the truck up next to the spot where the sewer construction had ended for the week. The hole blocked the road. "Enthusiasm or nuisance, take your pick," she said. "It depends on which side of the issue you're on."

"Don't you like her?" I asked, climbing out. For someone who was so obviously upset by her niece's disappearance, Vida seemed to have a very negative view of her.

"It's not a question of *like*. She has her good points and her bad points. Like you say, she's got a lot of drive. But she's not mature enough to focus all that energy. She goes from one cause to the next. It can be a nuisance. But that doesn't mean I don't love her. She is my only sister's—God rest her soul— daughter." Vida's voice trembled. "Vejay, I dropped her off at this anti-hookers' group meeting at St. Agnes' last night and she hasn't been home since. I don't know what to do."

I put my arm around Vida's shoulders and waited till her shaking stopped. Then we started up the stairs of Michelle's house.

"Have you called the hospitals, the highway patrol, the sheriff?" I asked.

"Craig called the hospitals three times, the last time right before he left for work this morning. He called the highway patrol and left a number. They said they'd let him know if they found Michelle. But they won't find her; she wasn't driving."

"She could have been riding with someone else," I said.

Vida walked across the deck and unlocked the door to Michelle and Craig's house. She motioned me into a large, paneled, and surprisingly empty room. "Michelle wasn't riding," she said. "I called Father Calloway at St. Agnes'. He dropped her off in town after the meeting."

"Well, what did the sheriff say?"

Vida stopped. "We didn't want to call the sheriff. Henderson is a small town."

"If a person's missing you call the sheriff."

She began to pace the length of the room. "Vejay, you know Sheriff Wescott. Maybe you could see if he's heard anything."

"Like what? Like he's found a body?" As soon as I said it I regretted it. "I'm sorry, Vida, but either Michelle is missing or she's not. If she's missing, you need the best help you can get."

She continued to pace. I had to strain to hear her. "We talked about that, Craig and me. But suppose Michelle comes home, suppose she spent the night with a friend and the phone went dead. Then next week we'd pick up the newspaper and there'd be a paragraph in the Sheriff's Report announcing that Michelle Davidson's husband reported her missing overnight. Regardless of the cause, everyone in town would be talking. Michelle would be humiliated, and she'd be furious. And it wouldn't be good for Craig's nursery business either." She took a breath. "I'm doing the best I can by asking you to help, Vejay. You've solved a murder. You know about these things."

"That investigation didn't win me any friends in town, or in the sheriff's department either." It had been only a few months ago when my friend Frank Goulet, the bartender at Frank's Place, was shot. I

was the last person seen there, a fact that had caused
the sheriff to view me with suspicion. I had searched
for Frank's murderer more to save myself than to
promote justice.

"Vejay." Vida's mouth trembled. I had never seen
her this upset.

Vida was our union representative. She had
fought to get me my pay for the days I'd been sus-
pended after my investigation of Frank's murder,
even though the preparations for the hearing had
taken more of her time than the total of the hours I
had been docked. It was Vida who was always ready
to listen to the rest of us meter readers, to hear our
gripes, to consider our problems. When I had had
the flu last winter it was she who brought me a
week's groceries and enough cold remedies to cure
all of Henderson. I owed Vida a lot. She was a good
friend—which made her anguish all the more dis-
tressing. I said, "Of course, I'll do whatever I can.
You know that. Tell me what you want."

"Just see what you can find out. Talk to the neighbors. Maybe they saw something. You can tell them
you're looking for Michelle and you can't get a hold
of her. That doesn't sound like her husband doesn't
know where she is."

There were two director's chairs in the room, the
only places to sit. I took one. "You drove Michelle
to this anti-hookers' meeting. Tell me about that."

Vida sat in the other chair, uncomfortably, as if it
took all her effort not to leap out of it and continue
to pace. "It's Michelle's latest cause. The group is
going to picket outside the Grove this weekend. Michelle said the prostitutes create a bad atmosphere
for children here. She even took her kids to her sister's in Santa Rosa." In spite of her agitation, there

was a weary annoyance in Vida's voice. "Michelle called me and asked if I could drive her to the meeting. Craig had their car."

"Did she say anything on the way there?"

"She might have intended to, but she didn't. The thing is, Vejay, I've kind of lost patience with Michelle. I know I shouldn't have. She doesn't have her own mother to talk to. But I've been busy. I've . . . I don't know. I've been short with her. And now she doesn't talk about her causes. Last night I was relieved that she didn't. I didn't want to hear about this silly group. In any case, she was all caught up in her ongoing row with her neighbor Ward over his cesspool."

"So you drove her to the meeting and left her off at St. Agnes'. You didn't drive her home, right?"

"No." There was a different quality to that word, a dead clunking sound. "I wish I had. I wish Father Calloway had driven her *home*. He dropped her at the bar in town. She saw a man she knew and told Father Calloway to let her off. She wouldn't have done that with me. Or at least I would have known who she was with."

Suddenly the reason for Michelle's disappearance, and Vida's mixed feelings, seemed clearer. "Vida," I said, "are you worried that Michelle went off with a lover for the night? Is that it? It's hardly uncommon here, particularly around Bohemian Week, with all the different men in town."

"No," she snapped. "No. Look, Vejay, Michelle is a good wife and mother. Her home is important to her. And she's all involved in the protest group. The demonstrations start tonight, for god's sake. She wouldn't just leave now, particularly to shack up with some guy."

It was like Vida to think that. A woman who refers to her niece as a pain in the behind isn't likely to picture that behind bare in bed with a stranger.

"Oh, Vejay, your beer," she said. "I promised you a beer. And lunch. You haven't had that." She jumped up, then paused, staring at the gold sunburst clock above the fireplace, the only decoration in the room. "Oh, it's almost one o'clock. I have to get back to work. I'm sorry about lunch. But there's bound to be beer in the fridge. You help yourself. And to lunch, too. It's the least we can offer you."

"Okay, but before you go, tell me, where is Craig?" Craig, who hadn't wanted to call the sheriff, also didn't seem to find his wife's disappearance sufficiently disturbing to keep him at home.

"He's at the nursery. Like he said, you can't leave a business to run itself. He's right—there's nothing he could do here. I told him to go on." She opened the door. "You've investigated things before, Vejay. You know what to do."

I had barely reiterated that I would do what I could when Vida rushed out the door. Left alone, I hardly knew where to begin.

I remembered Michelle. Even to beard the meter reader, she had put on makeup and clothes that were chosen to show off her figure. And in our brief conversations it was apparent to me that she wanted not only to know about her meter's reading, but she wanted my attention. Was she, as Vida suggested, bored? Was she looking for something to break the monotony? Michelle seemed like a young woman who could be enticed into a fling. Vida was sure Michelle wouldn't, but of course, decent young wives do have affairs. Nice girls with tired busy husbands and small children find other lifestyles seductive—find other men. And in Henderson, where in winter there is nothing more entertaining than a drive to the supermarket in Guerneville, people are thrown back on their own resources. I had spent many a winter's evening huddled near my fire reading. For those who didn't read there was television, the bars, and the lure of an illicit affair that gave one day a different meaning than the next.

It was now one P.M. Michelle Davidson was probably getting out of a rumpled bed in a motel in Jenner, where the Russian River exits into the Pacific, and wondering what she would tell Craig.

If Michelle Davidson had shacked up for the night, she might return any minute to find me going through her house—a distinctly unpleasant prospect no matter how I handled it.

So, I moved quickly through the dining area, which held only a redwood picnic table and four chairs. The kitchen was that of any young mother without gourmet aspirations. Cupboards were stocked with cereal boxes, macaroni and cheese, instant this and instant that. There were few ingredients per se, and none of those copper or enamel articles one sees in kitchen catalogs. I glanced in the drawers and under the sink, but there was nothing out of the ordinary there.

Skipping the children's rooms, I checked the master bedroom. On the dresser, framed in monogrammed silver, was Craig and Michelle's wedding picture. Craig, just a bit taller than Michelle, appeared mature, even staid, though at the time he couldn't have been more than twenty-five years old. He looked like a man who was born staid. And he looked unsure. I picked up the photo, holding it closer, trying to see into the faces. If Craig seemed apprehensive, the reason was obvious. Michelle, standing next to him, was tiny, but stunning. Her long dark hair was flipped back, à la Farrah

Fawcett. Her dark eyes glistened, and she smiled not at Craig, but at the camera.

Putting the picture back in place, I glanced around the room. A matching bedroom set dominated it. Two twelve-by-eighteen-inch frames held clusters of pictures of Michelle and the children, a boy and girl about five or six years old. Under them, on the nightstand, was a yearbook, Michelle's high school yearbook from eight years ago. Looking down at it I wondered what had become of mine. I didn't recall it amongst the carloads of belongings I had moved out of the San Francisco apartment after my divorce. Probably it was still in my parents' attic. In any case, it had never had a place on my nightstand. Perhaps college puts high school events in perspective. Or, more likely, my memories were not as glowing as Michelle's.

I opened the yearbook in the middle, and turned the pages slowly. Indeed, my memories were not of this caliber. Michelle was the girl we had all envied in those days. Her picture graced almost every page. She was shown leading the pompom squad, with the school service league, as queen of the senior prom. Half a page was devoted to shots of Michelle at a state gymnastics meet—midway through a flip off the uneven bars, at the high point of her vault over the horse, standing on one foot on the balance beam while bringing the other foot up behind her back to touch her head. In the final picture she was receiving a medal. She was a natural for gymnastics—tiny, strong, and beautiful. I wondered if she had gone on with her gymnastics after high school.

But perhaps involvement in causes had supplanted gymnastics. Stuck between the pages of the yearbook was a snapshot of Michelle and a tall wavy-haired young man at a demonstration. He towered over her, carrying a sign. She looked on. Was this the seed for her support of later causes, including the anti-hookers' group?

Replacing the yearbook, I glanced in the closet. Craig's clothes occupied a third, Michelle's the rest. And while his were mostly workclothes, Michelle's were designer jeans, silk blouses, and a three-foot-high pile of expensive bulky knit sweaters.

I looked around the room again, and checked the hall and living room on my way out. I had expected to find a desk or table or even a box, cluttered with papers, magic markers, picket sticks, the paraphernalia of the anti-hookers' group, but there was none of it. The house was spotless, as if Michelle had cleaned it just prior to her departure.

Having peered through Michelle's clothes, speculated on her marriage, riffled through her yearbook, I couldn't bring myself to raid her refrigerator. I would talk to the neighbor, the one with the cesspool, then I'd have lunch, and my beer.

I shut the front door and made my way down the stairs, avoiding a clump of ivy that trailed over two steps. At the bottom I turned back and looked up at the house. Like many of the newer hillside houses it was not painted, but stained wood. Its deck hung off the front, wide and pendulous, giving the whole structure the appearance that one good rain would wash it down the bare hillside and into the street. But it was sturdier than it looked. Homes here were built on supports sunk deep into the rocky hillside. Rains would come and the river would flood but the cabins and chalets on the hillside would survive. Still, there was something very impermanent about this house, Michelle and Craig's. It wasn't the struc-

ture, but the nearly bare earth outside and the
sparsely furnished rooms inside. It looked as if Michelle and Craig were still in the process of moving
in. Or moving out.

Below on North Bank Road came the sounds of
traffic—horns blaring, brakes squealing as the tourists headed through the heat of the afternoon
toward their vacation cabins or the town beach.

I walked around the garage and up ten stairs to
the neighbor's door. The house, older than the
Davidsons', was painted beige and trimmed in
French blue. There was no deck in front, but a porch
in the rear. These older houses were built closer into
the hillside. A wooden sign announced *The
McElveys'*. I knocked.

I had read the meter here, around back by the side
of the porch, but I had never seen either of the
McElveys at home. Ward McElvey I had met in
passing a few times when I had been working one of
the Guerneville routes. His realty company, Remson
Realty (Remson after the father-in-law who founded
it), had moved into Guerneville proper just before I
started with PG&E. I had seen the old storefront on
the outskirts of town that had housed the business
when Mr. Remson started it in 1953. Mostly, Mr.
Remson had handled the weekly or monthly rentals
that were the bread and butter of realtors then. But
the Remson Realty I saw these days was in one of
the newly constructed shingled buildings along the
main road leading from Santa Rosa to Guerneville.
No longer did Remson's handle the demanding
trade of weeklong rentals; now the colored photo-
graphs out front showed condos and duplexes for
sale at prices that would have made old Mr. Remson

spin. Ask about Sunset Villas, a sign in the window invited.

Ward McElvey opened his front door. He was middle-aged, five-foot-ten, with a solid but not heavy build and a square face. His brown hair had the fluff of blow-drying. He wore brown slacks and a white tennis sweater that was too heavy for the day. "What can I do for you?" he asked, ushering me into the foyer. After the heat outside it seemed invitingly cool in here.

I was surprised that he had let me in without an explanation. As a meter reader I was bonded. Customers knew that, but it rarely encouraged them to invite me into their homes. But perhaps Ward McElvey's reaction was not caused so much by my business as by his. Perhaps he viewed each stranger as a prospective home buyer.

"Mr. McElvey, I'm Vejay Haskell."

His eyes narrowed. I wondered if he were having second thoughts about letting me in.

"I know I've seen you in town," he said. "I just couldn't place your name. I'm sorry." He looked uncomfortable.

"You've met me reading your electric meter, so it's no wonder you don't know my name."

He looked down at my sweat-stained uniform.

"I'm not here on business," I added quickly.

"Ah, well," he said, apparently relieved, "then can I get you something to drink? A beer?"

I seemed to be perpetually offered beers I couldn't drink. "No, thanks."

"We were just having a drink before going out to the site," he said, taking me into the living room.

The walls were covered with paintings—abstract portraits, nudes, groupings—all huge, with huge faces in reds and browns, or navy and brown, or shades of greens that melted into one another. They so dominated the room that it was a moment before I noticed Ward McElvey's guests, an older city-dressed couple on a green brocade sofa.

"Mr. and Mrs. Underwood, this is Vejay Haskell." To me, he announced, "Mr. and Mrs. Underwood are here to see Sunset Villas, or more precisely, the attractive riverside location where our villas will be built."

Mr. Underwood seemed about to push himself up then decided against it. "How d'ya do?" he said. His wife merely nodded.

Before I could respond, McElvey continued. "Sunset Villas will offer a dream retirement for forty fortunate couples and a superb investment for forward-looking people." He smiled at the Underwoods. I felt sure I was being treated to a much-used sales pitch.

"We were just looking at one of the model units pictured here—"

"Mr. McElvey," I said.

"Ward."

"Ward. I hate to disturb you but I'm really just looking for your neighbor, Michelle Davidson."

"Oh, you are. Hmm. Well, anything I can do," he said with a clear lack of enthusiasm. To the Underwoods, he said, "If you folks will excuse us. You know where the bar is, so you help yourselves."

The Underwoods nodded slowly and I suspected that Ward McElvey had been helping them to drinks since they arrived. It explained Mr. Underwood's decision not to try standing up.

With their assurances that he was excused, Ward McElvey led me back into the hallway and leaned stiffly against the wall. In his sweater, he looked hot and uncomfortable. And now that the novelty of being out of the sun had worn off, I felt the heat inside too.

"What's this about Michelle?" he asked.

"I need to get in touch with her. I can't find her. She wasn't home last night. I just thought you might have seen her in the last day or two." Even to me my statement sounded disjointed. I hoped Ward McElvey wouldn't question my relationship to Michelle or why I needed to see her so urgently.

But he didn't. He glanced anxiously back toward the living room. "Her husband—"

"He wasn't much help. Maybe he's too busy. I just thought . . ." I let the words trail off, but gave no suggestion of leaving. I was beginning to see what a ridiculous position I had allowed myself to get into. How do you ask about someone you can't admit is missing?

Ward's mouth twitched, as if wavering between a variety of replies. Finally, he said, "You know, I did see her last night." Glancing back at the couple in the living room, he motioned me a few steps further into the hallway and said softly, "You work for PG and E. You know about the sewer."

The sewer was in no way connected to the electric company, but as a homeowner, I knew as much as the next person about the sewer project that had run millions of dollars and several years over estimate. It promised to be completed soon. After all, the sewer pipe had made it through town and as far as this street.

"I know about the sewer." Adding to the fiction of my friendship with Michelle, I said, "Michelle told me about your cesspool."

"She did? Well, that's what she was carrying on about last night. She's probably told everyone in town. She even threatened to complain to her congressman. I said I was sorry about the mosquito larvae. No one wants them on their garage wall. I didn't let my leach lines work their way there on purpose, you know."

Cesspools and septic tanks were elements of rusticity I hadn't been prepared for when I had moved here from San Francisco. But I learned all too quickly. Cesspools were wooden boxes; septic tanks were larger cement cylinders with one or two compartments. Both took care of the solid material. The liquid was carried out of them and into the ground by underground fingers of gravel called leach lines. Initially, the water drained only to the ends of the leach lines, but over the years the force of the water or the vagaries of the soil and rock changed or extended the flow till it came to a wall, or a stream—or in this case, Michelle Davidson's garage.

"What Michelle has leaking into her garage isn't pure sewage, but it's not something she would want next to her car window either, is it?" I asked.

"Well, no. I tried to be reasonable. It's not a disaster. I offered to come in and scoop up the mess. I would have done that. But, well, you know Michelle."

"How *did* she react?"

"Like she always does. You can imagine the magnitude she's blown it into, can't you? Last night's tirade was standard. She's gotten so bad that I never go out without checking to see if she's there. I have to park my car down the street, and when I leave the house, I use the back door and skirt around behind the people on the far side and down through their property."

"Wouldn't it be easier to deal with the cesspool?"

He put a hand on my shoulder. "You'd think, but the thing is—I've explained this to Michelle, but you know how she is—the sewer will be in shortly. You can see the hole right in front of my garage, so even if I wanted to park there I couldn't. Anyway, when the sewer is in, there will be a hook-up charge."

I nodded. I knew that only too well.

"And the question is, how much will it cost, right? It's based on how many people hook in, right? If it's reasonable, I'll hook in. If not, I'll get a septic tank. But, as I've told Michelle over and over, I'm not going to get a septic tank now if there's a chance I'll hook into the sewer in a month. That's reasonable, isn't it?"

I nodded again.

He gave my shoulder a squeeze and released it, an affectation I found increasingly irritating. "Tell that to Michelle," he said. "She's called the county; she called Mosquito Abatement. Environmental Health sent a man out. She called the county again. They called me. You know Michelle; when she gets on a jag like this she never lets go." He took another step into the hallway. "I'll tell you what I think, Vejay. I think Craig Davidson spends too much time at his nursery and Michelle just doesn't have enough to do with her time."

I was tempted to comment that no amount of work or time spent on hobbies would make sewage leaking into your garage acceptable. Instead, I asked, "Do you have any idea, anything at all, about where she might be?"

"Maybe she went off with the Environmental

Health man." He laughed. "No. I don't want to say anything out of line. But Michelle is a very attractive girl. She knows it, too. She's particularly attractive if she doesn't open her mouth. To a guy in a bar . . . well, you know what I mean." He smiled conspiratorially. "Doesn't dress like a nun, either, up there on her deck railing in a leotard."

That railing was two and a half feet above the deck. From it the drop to the ground was anywhere from ten to twenty-five feet. "What was she doing up there?"

He shrugged. "Walking. Sometimes backwards. One time she did a back roll. She knows how to show off her best features, if you know what I mean."

Ignoring that observation, I asked, "Do you think your wife might have talked to Michelle recently?"

Ward glanced toward the living room. "My guests," he said in way of explanation. "Jenny? I doubt it. You probably don't know Jenny."

"No, I don't think so." I might have seen her or spoken to her, but I didn't connect any particular woman to this house.

"She does those little sketches on the sidewalk downtown. You know, the souvenir pictures the summer people buy."

"Oh yes, I have seen her there. She's very good."

He nodded absently. "She may know something about Michelle, but I doubt it. She doesn't like to be bothered, particularly by Michelle. But you can ask her."

"Why particularly by Michelle?"

He looked again toward the living room. "My guests . . . I really can't leave them any longer, you understand. They're anxious to get out to the site."

"But why particularly Michelle?"

He shrugged. "Jenny doesn't have much patience."

That didn't answer my question, but I couldn't ask again. Instead, I asked to use his phone.

"Certainly," he said with clear relief. "Right back in the bedroom. Let yourself out when you're through." He patted my shoulder again—I restrained comment, again—and he hurried back to the living room.

I sat on the bed, pulled the phone book out from under the phone, and looked up the number for Craig's nursery. Sitting there with my finger marking it, I wondered why Ward's wife found Michelle especially offensive. It didn't sound like she was a protagonist in the cesspool dispute. Was the problem something entirely different? Was it Michelle's not dressing like a nun, as Ward put it? Did she suspect Ward's wandering hands had found their way to Michelle's body?

Outside the window, on the porch, was a tall man with light curly hair leaning against the railing, staring down thoughtfully into the underbrush. Was he another of Ward McElvey's prospects? Or perhaps the neighbor whose yard Ward cut through? He looked familiar, or almost familiar. But I saw so many people in my work that I recognized people I didn't really know.

Changing my mind about calling Michelle's husband now, I put the phone book back. It was nearly two o'clock. Lunch first, then Craig.

Ward and the Underwoods were still in the living room. I caught his eye and waved as I left.

Stepping from the house into the sunlight was like walking into a sauna. I forced myself to hurry down the stairs, and along the street. As I passed the next house, I noted a red AMC Pacer with license plates saying MCELVEY.

It wasn't till I was halfway down the hill that I realized who the man outside Ward McElvey's reminded me of—the man with Michelle in the photo I'd found between the pages of her yearbook.

Even in the shade of the eucalyptus trees it was much too hot. My polyester uniform slacks were like sweat pants. My shirt clung to my back. I was only pleased that it was just two blocks into town.

Michelle Davidson's street, Half Hill Road, ran high above and parallel to the river. It ended at Zeus Lane, so named because it rose straight up to the gods, or viewed from the top, steeply down toward town. The one advantage of being dressed in work clothes was that my boots were made for clambering up driveways and through underbrush to the obscure places builders chose to put meters. Walking down a slope was child's play.

As I skirted from shady spot to shady spot I wondered who the man behind Ward McElvey's house, the man in Michelle's picture, was. More to the point, what was he doing next to Michelle's house the day after her disappearance? Had she gone off with him and then sent him back for her clothes? If so, why was he sitting on Ward's porch instead of walking in Michelle's door? Surely she would have given him the key. But perhaps I had caught him while he was waiting to make sure the house was empty. I hadn't wanted to run into Michelle inside her house. How much more would her lover do to avoid a confrontation with Craig there?

But that was speculation. First I needed to find out

who the man was. And even before that I needed lunch. I hurried on down to North Bank Road and along the sidewalk toward the café.

One of the things I had gained since becoming a meter reader was an enormous appetite. I walked more in a week now than I had in a year as an account executive in San Francisco. If I ever stopped reading meters, I'd either have to go on a hunger strike or seek work with the circus. But for now I just hoped it was too hot for tourists to think of food.

I was wrong. The café was jammed. Every stool at the counter was taken, every table crowded, and there was a line waiting to get in. In disgust I stomped across the street to Fischer's Ice Cream and joined the line there. The Fischers had run the shop for years and they moved the line through with a speed any bank would have envied. There were five flavors a day and by the time you reached the front of the line, you were expected to have your choice ready. Mine was strawberry, double-scoop. It would do for an appetizer.

Cone in hand, I wandered along the sidewalk, skirting toddlers, jumping back to avoid a boy in cutoffs who was backing toward my cone. At the far end of the sidewalk was a beach umbrella, and under it, I made out as I neared, was a woman sketching. Presumably, she was Jenny McElvey.

I had seen her there before, but I had never taken the time to look closely at her work. Today the subject of that work, a man in his early twenties, sat on a folding chair, staring tensely to one side of Jenny. He looked edgy and self-conscious, as if he were sitting there on a bet. The corners of his mouth seemed about to break into a nervous grin. I glanced from him to the sketch. Nearly done, it approximated his features but missed the singular qualities that would have transformed it from a likeness of a pale young man into a portrait of this particular one. Still, there was a certain flair to it, perhaps the angle of the head, or the thick definite strokes that seemed fitting for a charcoal sketch acquired while on vacation.

I moved around behind the man so I could watch Jenny. She looked to be a little younger than I, probably about thirty. Her brown hair was drawn back at the neck, folded over and clasped up on her head, so that none of it hung against her neck. Her face was bare of any makeup. Her eyebrows were thick and seemed to have grown randomly. But her eyes, large and dark brown, stared fiercely at the paper, moving only briefly to view the subject.

Abruptly she put down the charcoal, and without an appraising glance, handed the paper to the young man. She looked exhausted, like a psychic recently revived from a trance.

I glanced at the crowd, expecting the man's friends to push forward to get their money's worth of amusement, but no one elbowed in. The crowd as a whole moved closer and their murmurs of approval bubbled up. The man himself gave the drawing all the careful evaluation that Jenny had not. Finally, he smiled, and returned it to her to be wrapped. The crowd stood a minute or so, apparently waiting to see if another subject would take his place. When none did, individuals and small groups wandered off. The man stepped up to Jenny, extricated a bill from his wallet, and accepted the drawing.

A couple walked up, glanced at me, and moved on.

"Are you trying to decide?" Jenny asked me.

"No, actually, I'm looking for your neighbor, Michelle Davidson."

"She's not here." Jenny adjusted the sketch paper in its clasp. Clearly, to her the subject was closed. She wasn't even curious as to why I couldn't find Michelle or why I was bringing my problem to her.

"I've been looking for her since last night. I talked to your husband." I hesitated, then decided to plunge in. "He said you particularly disliked her."

"And so you figure I'll know where she is?" There was a mixture of irony and irritation in her voice.

"Actually, I thought you might be pretty straightforward."

She fingered the charcoal. "*Straightforward* is that you're hurting my business. People don't come to watch me talk, they're attracted by seeing me draw. Either you want a picture, or leave the space for someone else."

Again, I hesitated. I hated to invest more than time in Michelle's whereabouts. But I did like the idea of having my picture done, so I said, "Let me finish my cone, and then do a sketch of me. Okay?"

"Okay."

"But while I'm eating answer my questions."

"An eight-dollar interrogation?" she said with the barest hint of amusement.

"Only partly. It will be a treat for me to have the picture. I remember watching artists doing sketches and caricatures when I was a kid. I always wanted one, but it was a lot of money then."

Jenny smiled tentatively. It didn't seem like a normal expression for her. "Okay then, ask your questions, but you've got to keep licking that cone."

I sat in the chair. "Do you have any idea where Michelle could be? Father Calloway of St. Agnes' dropped her in town last night. I can't find out what happened after that."

Jenny leaned back in her chair. She eyed a couple walking by, then forced her attention back to me. "I haven't seen Michelle in days. I've been in Santa Rosa getting supplies. This is my busiest time. I do more work during Bohemian Week than the rest of the season combined. I have to make sure I have everything I need. I can't take a day off to run to Santa Rosa and pick up charcoal."

I looked at the sketch pad, the charcoal, the floodlight for evening work lying next to the easel. "It took you more than one trip to get your supplies?" I asked in amazement.

"Are you an artist? Do you know what decisions I have to make or how many places I have to go to get the best?"

I decided not to deal with that. "When was the last time you saw Michelle?"

She rubbed a finger along a piece of charcoal. "Look, the woman lives next door. She's part of the landscape. I can't remember when she was out on her deck, doing her Olga Korbut number on the railing. Like Ward was kind enough to tell you, Michelle and I are not friends."

I had the feeling that Jenny McElvey was on the verge of deciding that an empty chair was preferable to me. "Your husband Ward was talking to Michelle last night, about the cesspool." I paused, but she didn't react to that. "He was as helpful as he could be, but I obviously caught him at a time when he had a lot to do."

"I'm sure," she said with the same bitterness she'd had for Michelle. "Look, this is the most important time of the year for me. If anyone ever discovers me as an artist tucked away in the country it will happen during Bohemian Week when all the bigshots and reporters and people with taste and influence are here. Ward knows that. So what does he do? Does he try to make things easier for me? Does he offer to take my part-time job at the nursery? No. What he does is invite a pair of total strangers for the weekend. They came yesterday. And they're staying till Sunday night. He wants the house clean; he wants me to go to dinner with them. He's angry that I won't stay home and amuse them. *He's* angry!" She was shaking.

I sat, amazed by the vehemence of her outburst.

A group of four paused, looking from Jenny to me and back to her. Then, seeing that no sketch was in progress, they moved on.

"I guess Michelle's anti-hookers' group won't help your business, or anyone else's either," I said.

It was a moment before Jenny answered. She seemed to be recovering from her outburst. When she did speak, her tone was almost indifferent. "It won't affect my business. It's a silly little group, headed by a silly young woman. It's not going to impress the hookers or their customers. Michelle just wants to get her picture in the paper."

In spite of her bitterness toward Ward, I still wondered if her reaction to Michelle was based on jealousy. I asked, "Why do you dislike Michelle?"

She took a moment before answering. "I don't really dislike her, because I don't really know her.

But I find her actions a constant nuisance. Ask anyone who lives near her, they'll know what I mean.
Right now we have a sewer hole blocking our garage. That's because Michelle kept bugging the city
council to keep on the sewer company. If she had let
things run their course it wouldn't have gotten there
till fall when the town wasn't so mobbed and we
wouldn't have tourists driving up the street, slamming on their brakes at the hole, and then trying to
turn around. We've almost had our car hit three or
four times."

"Surely that's not the only reason."

"No, it's just the latest. I've known Michelle since
she was a child. She's four years younger than I am.
When she was in high school my brother Ross took
her out from time to time. He was already out of
school—a big man. He'd invite her somewhere
when the spirit moved him, then he'd forget about
her. And she'd come over to the house looking for
him. I sort of felt sorry for her—it was lousy of Ross
—but at the same time she was such a pest. She was
a very popular girl, and she just couldn't accept that
someone she wanted didn't care about her."

Thinking of the picture inside Michelle's yearbook, I asked, "What does Ross look like?"

"I don't know."

"Ross—your brother."

"I said I don't know. I haven't seen him in eight
years, since my father died. He left town that day.
My father had a heart attack. He had it because he
was shoveling a hole and Ross was standing by
watching him work—and there you have Ross's
character in a nutshell." She swallowed. "Ross
didn't even bother to come to the hospital. Ward
had to ride in the ambulance with my father. And

when I looked for Ross to drive me there, he was gone. He just left."

"Where is he now?"

"I don't know. He lived in San Francisco, off some woman. That was years ago. He hasn't come back. I wouldn't see him if he did." She looked down at the charcoal and when she looked at me again she seemed to be in control. "I'm sure I sound spiteful but if you knew Ross you wouldn't be surprised. He came and went as he pleased. But there was always a job for him with my father. My father kept thinking it would work out, that Ross would shape up and take over the business, like a son should. It was lucky for him that he had Ward to get some work done. Ross was too busy with himself. He had to go to Mexico, or he had to picket at the Grove, or ride his motorcycle. He was always too busy to take customers around. Ward had to do that. Or my father. It's no wonder he had a heart attack."

I waited a moment before asking, "When you saw him last, was Ross tall with sandy hair?"

She nodded.

"There's a snapshot Michelle has of herself and a tall sandy-haired man holding a picket sign . . ."

She nodded again. "Michelle showed it to me. She'd brought it to show to Ross, but, of course, he wasn't there. That picture was the story of their relationship—Ross looking at the sign, Michelle staring cow-eyed at Ross."

"That was definitely Ross in the picture?" I could hear the excitement creep into my voice.

"Yes. Of course. Why?"

"Because I saw him on the back porch of your

house today. It might not have been him, but it looked a lot like—"

The charcoal snapped. Jenny sat staring at it. I couldn't decide by looking at her if her reaction was shock, or anger, or both.

"If Ross came back, would Michelle have spent the night with him?"

Her eyes refocused slowly. "What?"

I repeated the question.

In that time she gathered herself together. "Probably," she snapped. "If he'd asked her to walk barefoot to Nome she would have done that. And that's—"

"Jenny." A couple was standing beside the easel. I hadn't noticed them. I was sure Jenny hadn't either. The man continued, "I really want a picture of my girl. Are you going to be through soon?"

"Yes. I'm through now."

"What about my picture?" I said.

"You got what you wanted. Now leave me to do my work." The bitterness in her voice put me in a group with Ross and Michelle.

I got up, leaving the chair to the girlfriend. As I walked along the sidewalk toward my house, I wondered, if his sister hated Ross, how would Craig Davidson feel?

CHAPTER

4

Ross Remson was the man in the snapshot with Michelle, but was he the man on Ward and Jenny's porch? Or was that man just someone who resembled Ross? If only I had looked more closely at the man's face in the snapshot rather than Michelle's. I could recall it only generally. I needed to see that picture again before the memory of the man behind the McElveys' faded. And I needed to ask Ward who that man was.

Now I hurried through town, glancing irritably into the still-crowded café. Lunch would have to come from my own fridge. I skirted the families that sauntered along the sidewalk, blocking wide swaths of it with their beach bags and hampers and piles of blankets. The children ran ahead urgently, calling to their laden parents to hurry; every moment on the beach was precious. I maneuvered around them and rushed on across the street just as the light—Henderson's one traffic light—turned red.

My house was three blocks beyond. In the heat of the afternoon it seemed like three miles. Still, I did have the afternoon off from work; I wasn't edging past a snarling dog that might not have been vaccinated to get to a meter behind a prickly pyracantha bush. In a few minutes my soaked and none-too-fragrant uniform would be on the laundry pile and a meatloaf sandwich that would satisfy any construction worker would be on my plate. And I finally would have my long-awaited beer.

Half an hour later, having showered, changed into jeans and a T-shirt, and dialed both Michelle's and Ward's phone numbers while I ate (no answer from either one), I climbed down the sloping Z of steps from my house. I backed my pickup out of the garage and headed through town again.

This was as ready as I would be to face the unpleasant task of talking to Craig Davidson, Michelle's husband. It would have been appealing to put it off, but I needed to see Ross's picture again, and to know if any of Michelle's clothes had been removed since I'd been in the house. So I had to get the house key from Craig. When I asked for it he would doubtless want to know what I had found out and I would have to tell him that I suspected his wife might have run off with Ross.

It was a bit after three when I pulled into the lot of Davidson's Plants. The building, a twenty-by-forty prefab structure, was located on a sixty-foot-square lot at the west end of the commercial block of Henderson. Most of the town was either hillside or low enough to be washed out in heavy spring flooding every few years; finding a level spot that was high enough to escape the smaller floods was an accomplishment in itself. Craig's nursery probably escaped the waters all but once a decade.

I walked through the open sliding doors. Craig Davidson was behind the counter. He was a short man with the wiry muscular body of one who unloads bags of manure off of trucks and moves potted azaleas around a store. His brown hair had been bleached by the sun and hung a bit below his ears. It was not quite sand-colored, not quite wavy, but almost. Looking at him, I wondered if he did not quite measure up to Ross. I wondered if Michelle felt that way, if she had actually thought it, and if Craig knew. Or if the whole comparison existed only in my mind.

The interior of the shop was divided into three sections. The far side held the plastic bags of potting soil, vermiculite, and peat moss, and the boxes of plant food and snail pellets that only made the race to gobble down tender sprouts more of a challenge for the hearty California snail. The middle section sported a display of indoor plants—false aralias, wandering Jews, coleus, various fig trees, decorative cacti, and an array of succulents. And nearer the door was the counter where Craig stood dealing with the first of a line of six customers—a man in dirt-streaked Levi's, a workshirt that should have been washed months ago (if not thrown out), and work boots. His long tangled beard melded with his unkempt hair. Clearly he belonged in the hills, shooting squirrels, growing marijuana, or living off a veteran's pension, not standing in line in a plant shop clutching the least appealing African violet from the display next to the counter. He looked wary and uncomfortable.

It was a look shared by the other customers, who had backed away from him.

He pushed the African violet toward Craig.

It was then that the stench of new perspiration on his sweat-stained shirt hit me. No wonder the other customers had backed off. I edged away. Even Craig appeared uneasy as he muttered something to the man and hurriedly made change.

Next in line was a painfully thin woman with limp blond hair and the unmistakable rash of poison oak on both arms. Poison oak was ever-lurking in the Henderson underbrush, growing around the foundations of houses, or carried in liquid form on the fur of dogs who had rolled in that brush. I had taken the ImunOak PG&E gave us, but I still kept a safe distance.

When the man picked up his drooping African violet and headed for the door, I pushed in front of the woman.

"Hey, what are you—"

"Craig," I said, before the woman could continue, "I'm Vejay Haskell, the woman Vida told you would be calling this morning."

He looked momentarily confused, then said, "Yes, of course," in almost a whisper.

"Can I talk to you a minute?"

He stared at the line of customers. "My assistant, Alison, isn't here now. She's out in the truck. People are waiting. I can't just—"

"I need to check something in your house."

"Oh?" His voice was so low that it sounded as if it were caught in his beard. His tanned face, which had been scrunched with foreboding, relaxed. He caught my eye and smiled, a little-boy smile that transformed him from the staid man of the wedding picture into an appealing sprite. "The house keys are in the truck, I'm afraid."

"Don't you have a set here?"

"No, sorry. The only keys are in the truck. I don't need them till the end of the day, and by then the truck is back, you see."

"Where is the truck?"

"Let me check for you?" He turned to the woman with the poison oak, favoring her with the same smile. "Will you excuse me just a moment Mrs.

Frederick? I'll be right with you. Those fuchsias should do well on your deck." He waited till she smiled in acknowledgment and then disappeared into the office behind the counter.

I didn't look at the woman with the poison oak or the customers behind her, but I could feel their hostility. Not only was I making them wait, but I was creating a problem for their Craig.

"It's number seven forty-three out on Route One-Sixteen. Alison was planning to be there an hour. You should be able to catch her if you hurry," he said.

"Thanks."

"Sure." He turned back to Mrs. Frederick. As he took the plants from her, I noticed that Craig showed none of the wariness of coming near her rash that I had felt.

I walked back to my pickup, trying to settle on a clear opinion of Craig. Obviously he was busy. And he had an undeniable charm and pleasant manner with his customers and even with me, whom he didn't want to see. But his wife had been missing for nearly twenty-four hours, and for whatever reason —fear of what I might tell him, inability to make his customers wait, or just disinterest—he hadn't even asked what I had discovered. I wondered if Michelle's absence was not as uncommon an event as Vida believed it to be. After all, Michelle had taken her children to Santa Rosa. Perhaps she knew that Ross was coming to town. Perhaps this was not the first time. Perhaps Ross was not the only man. Of course, it was also possible that the man behind Ward McElvey's house was not Ross.

I climbed into the pickup, backed out, and headed across town once more.

Route 116 was on the far side of the river, through Guerneville. It ran from the woodsy river area south through small cattle and sheep farms to family orchards and the villages amongst them, and finally to Sebastopol and the freeway that led to San Francisco. There was a move afoot to have it declared a scenic route.

But the house outside which the Davidson's Plants truck was parked was not going to help in that effort. It was a small, white-shingled rectangle with no distinguishing marks set on a surprisingly flat parcel of land. In the yard a seedling stood unprotected, and around the walkway was turned earth. Alison Barluska, Craig's assistant, bent over the soil, scooping out a handful. A box of nitrogen additive sat to one side of her, a flat of impatiens to the other.

I had met Alison Barluska only once, at Vida's house. She was a slim but sturdy woman of about my own age. Now, through her shirt, I could see the ridges of her back muscles. As she turned toward me, I noted again the exotic quality of her face. Everything about it seemed just a bit extra. Her eyes were dark blue, large and set a smidgeon too far apart. Her eyebrows were thick. Her long dark blond hair was neither curly nor bushy, but full and undisciplined enough that it refused to stay behind her ears, and even as she bent back over the plants she kept pushing it out of her face with a soil-smudged hand.

"Alison, I'm here about Michelle," I said. "You do know she's missing, don't you? Vida asked me to check into it."

She nodded, sending a clump of hair into her face. Then she jerked her head and flung the hair back over her shoulder.

"I just talked to Craig." I recounted the conversation.

"How is he holding up?"

"He seemed disinterested."

She rested her hand on her trowel. "He was very upset this morning. He's been busy. The store is a zoo from Friday through Sunday. He needs someone to man the cash register. I should rearrange my days so I can be there on weekends. But some people want their work done on certain days. You know how it is."

"Not really."

Alison stood up. Even in dirt-streaked overalls she looked stylish. She was not pretty—none of her features was small enough to give her that little-girl look embodied in prettiness—but she had an air of confidence, like someone born to wealth. Had she wandered into a wedding reception dressed in her overalls, it would have been the bride who felt overdressed.

"We have a gardening service," she said. "That's why Craig hired me, to start it up. I canvass for it one day a week, and now spend three days doing the actual work. I'm only in the shop one day. Not much help to Craig."

I thought of my own steep yard, with its mixture of ivy, oxalis, general underbrush, and, of course, poison oak. It was standard for the Russian River area. "I shouldn't think there would be much call for landscaping here."

"You and everyone else. That's been my biggest problem—convincing people their yards could look better, or they could enjoy plants on their decks. We do a lot of work for absentee landlords who don't want to worry about whether their tenants will keep

their places up. Even the most responsible tenant
may not have the same taste as the owner. With us,
the landlords tell us what they want and we do it.
And then, also, they don't have to worry about the
tenants deducting 'expenses' from their rent. And
they don't have enthusiastic amateurs making mistakes."

"Should I assume that is your sales pitch? I used
to work in public relations; I know one when I hear
it."

"It's the openers—what I say in our letter to the
owners. This service is my baby. Craig thought it
was a good idea, but the operation is mine."

"You mean you proposed the whole idea?"

"Right. I wanted a job and Craig hadn't considered the need for a gardening service any more than
you have. It's been good for both Craig and me. He
gets money and publicity; I have a job where I can
be outside, work my own hours, and deal as I wish
with people. I sell people a good service for a reasonable cost."

"But you mostly work on rental properties?"

"Right. First I got a list of the absentee landlords
and sent them the letter. Then I called. After I'd
exhausted that list I canvassed door-to-door. That's
where I am now."

"Hard work."

"I don't mind it. I'm good at meeting lots of people. I've traveled around and I'm used to that kind
of thing." She bent down and began patting the
earth around a small plant. "I have to get this place
done in half an hour if I'm going to keep on sched-
ule. You don't mind." It was a statement rather than
a question.

I watched as Alison stood and hoisted a bag of

manure. She scooped out a bit, added it to the soil and mixed it in, then created a tiny crater for the plant.

"You must have given Michelle's disappearance some thought," I began. "Do you have any theories?"

Still looking at the soil, she said, "I don't know Michelle to speak of. I've met her only a couple times, and those were at the shop."

"Do you know if she's ever done anything like this before?"

"No."

"No she didn't, or no, you don't know?"

"I don't know."

"Craig never mentioned anything?"

"No."

I couldn't tell whether Alison was merely concentrating on her work, whether she was tired of talking, or whether she was intentionally not telling me something I needed to know. I decided on the more direct approach. "Did Craig ever mention an old boyfriend of Michelle's?"

Alison laughed.

It was not the response I had expected.

"Ross?"

"Yes. So Craig did talk about him?"

Alison turned, still squatting, and sat back on her heels. "Ross got me my job, in a sense."

"I didn't realize Ross had kept in touch with Craig."

"He hasn't. I'd better backtrack. I met Ross when I lived in San Francisco. He lived with me for about six months. And he talked about Henderson."

"Did he mention Michelle?"

"He said there was a high school girl who had the hots for him. That's all."

"And Craig?"

"Ross knew Craig. I had the impression then that everyone knew Craig."

"Was Ross surprised when Craig married Michelle?"

"That never came up."

"How did he get you the job? Did he call Craig?"

She laughed again. "No, no. I haven't seen Ross in years. What I mean by him getting me the job was that he brought me up to Henderson once years ago. As a matter of fact, that's how our relationship ended. He brought me up here for a weekend. We stayed in one of those lopsided motels by the river, you know, the ones with the plaid bedspreads that always have cigarette burns and the indoor-outdoor carpet that looks like it's been left outdoors until you checked in."

"Right, the Cozy Cabins."

"We stayed there Saturday night, and Sunday we went to the town beach. And then in the afternoon Ross said he had to deal with some family business. So he left me at the beach. It was about two o'clock. He never came back to the beach or the motel. And the next morning I left."

"Weren't you worried? Didn't you try to find him?"

She shrugged. "No. I figured something came up. It wasn't entirely out of character for Ross. And I didn't know where his family was or if there was some kind of family hassle I didn't want to get involved in. I figured then that he would come back to San Francisco and explain."

It fitted Alison to assume Ross could take care of himself. "Did he come back?" I asked.

"No. It was sort of odd. We were living together at the time. Or that's how I viewed it. But when Ross didn't come back, I realized that we were not so much living together as Ross had been staying with me. When I went to get rid of his stuff there was less than a cardboard box of it. And none of that was of any value."

"So what do you think happened to him?"

She shrugged. "For a while I figured something more attractive came up. But the more I thought about Ross, the more I realized he had been increasingly jumpy before we came up here. The guys he saw in San Francisco were none too reputable. We'd had a couple of fights because I didn't like them coming to my apartment. So, at first I thought he just wanted to be rid of me. Then it occurred to me that it was them he wanted to get distance from."

"Do you think he decided to move back here?"

"No. If they were after him he would have had to move farther. He probably planned on laying low on one of the marijuana farms north of here, or somewhere like that. Ross had a lot of connections here, some shadier than others. You know what this area is. There's a lot of illegal stuff going on. And then there's all the stuff connected with Bohemian Week. Ross called himself 'the Bohemian Connection.'"

"What does that mean?"

A sports car sped by, blaring music made undiscernible by its speed. Billows of dust flew up from the roadside. Alison rubbed the dust from her eyes, then pushed her hair back behind her ears. I repeated my question.

"I think Ross was mostly a gofer for the guys who needed quasi-legal arrangements for their employers, like places to meet prostitutes."

"Those places are called bars and motels."

"Not everyone can take the chance of being seen in a motel, even a discreet motel, particularly if the prostitute is of the same sex."

"Ah."

"Anyway, Ross made it sound like a big deal. And he probably did have connections here. And probably one of those guys he met through his gofering was willing to take him to his dope farm, or maybe he met someone who knew of someone who was running drugs from Mexico. That would be Ross's style."

"Did you meet any of his connections that weekend?"

"I might have. I remember a couple of rather shady types, but I don't know if they were involved in anything truly illegal or were just garden variety ne'er-do-wells. We seem to have a lot of those."

Like the people who cheat on their electricity usage, but not carefully enough to avoid being caught, I thought. "Would you say it was not out of the question for Ross to have come back and seen Michelle and invited her to leave with him now?"

"Not at all. That's exactly Ross. Enough time has passed so he'd feel safe surfacing again. But if that's what happened, Michelle will be back in a day or a week, or maybe a month or two, depending on how long it takes Ross to find something more interesting."

"You know," I said, "from what I hear of Ross and not just your description, the odd thing is that he would have friends at all."

She pushed herself up and started for the truck.

"I guess it does sound like that," she said, leaning against the driver's door. "I've told you Ross's failings. I thought that's what you wanted to know. But Ross was charming in his way. He was totally caught up in what was happening now. If he was with you, you were his entire focus. If he was involved in a project, that's what he talked about. And while he was doing it he was totally committed, completely reliable. And then, suddenly, it was over. It wasn't that he lost interest; it was like he never knew it existed."

"Still, that would make one a bit wary."

"It sounds like it when you're not involved, but it took a while to see that pattern. The first couple of times it happened, particularly if the subject was not yourself, it didn't register, or the change was so abrupt, so unusual in the normal day-to-day life, that you assumed you must have missed something. And while you were the subject of Ross's attention the intensity was so great, so flattering, that it was worth any effort to get it back."

"Then how come you just went back to the city when Ross didn't come back?"

"Well, Vejay, I was never a consuming passion for Ross. I always knew he was living with me temporarily."

"Really?" It was hard to imagine confident Alison on the short end of any relationship. Alison, who had come here knowing no one, who had talked her way into a job that seemed as unpromising as selling sand to a sheik and was making a go of it. I couldn't picture her letting Ross move in when he found her second-class. But women do a lot of less-than-well-adjusted things for lovers. My friends had done them. I had. I hoped I had outgrown doing them. I waited to see where Alison placed herself on this continuum.

But she added nothing. Instead, she reached into the truck and handed me Craig's house key.

"You never did tell me how Ross got you your job," I said.

She took a step back toward her plants. "Partly it was that Ross told me about the area, so I had an idea what kind of gardening service would be needed; partly that I told Craig that Ross had left me stranded here, and that appealed to Craig—hearing about Ross doing something rotten. It probably made a nice change." She gave me a quick dismissive nod of the head, a regal pronouncement that the audience was over, and returned to her plants.

I drove back across the Guerneville bridge and on toward Henderson. The windows of my pickup were all open, but that only served to channel the hot air. Outside I could hear the yelps and screams from the Guerneville beach. Had I looked down while crossing the bridge I could have seen the canoes passing under in either direction. Canoes were rented out at the beach. Upstream were islands, piles of sand raised a foot or two above the water line, where you could pull the canoe up and lie in the sun. Or you might eat salmon salad and watch the canoeists—parents paddling a child perched on the middle seat, divorced fathers with weekend children, couples, pairs of bare-bottomed guys who assumed their canoe seats were lower than they really were. At one spot above Guerneville the river was deep enough to allow a rope to fling any taker Tarzan-like into the water. But mostly the water was so shallow that the danger in canoeing was scraping the bottom of the boat.

Fifteen minutes later I drove through Henderson and up past the nursery to Half Hill Road. The area looked exactly as it had when I left about two hours ago. There were no vehicles parked either in front of the Davidsons' or the McElveys'. Surely if he were home, Ward McElvey would have parked in front.

He wouldn't drag his city prospects up the hill and through the neighbor's back yard.

I looked more closely at his house. The windows were shut. It was now four o'clock, traditionally the hottest hour of the day, and it had to be over one hundred degrees. The normal temperature was fifteen to twenty degrees cooler, with the Pacific breeze keeping things tolerable, and the redwoods and eucalyptus shading the roofs. But even they were no match for today's heat. No one would be home with their windows shut.

I pulled the truck up next to the sewer hole and made my way around it. Even though there was no sewage in it, nothing to distinguish it from any other fifteen-foot hole, I, like everyone else in town, gave it a wide berth, not really believing there was no raw sewage in there waiting to foul the feet of the unwary.

Once on Michelle's deck, I knocked before using the key. But no one was home here either. I went directly to the bedroom and found the picture in Michelle's album. In it, she stood, eight years ago, looking up at a tall young man with sandy hair. He held the picket sign. The sign was at an angle to the camera and the words were unclear. But what needed no interpretation was the adoration in Michelle's eyes.

I looked closely at Ross. His charm wasn't immediately apparent. But I could see the intensity Alison had described. He was tall and very thin. There was a space between his front teeth that made him look a little younger and more vulnerable. His hair was a bit curly, a bit long, a bit uncared for, as if he had no time for such inessentials. But as he looked toward the sign, his eyes were piercing. He held it with both hands, his arms stretched away from his body like he was making a religious offering. And yet there was something in his relation to the sign that focused the viewer's attention not on it but back to him. Michelle stared at him; the sign reflected him. He was the center of the snapshot.

But with the picture in front of me, I couldn't be sure this was the man I had seen next door earlier. It was, after all, eight years old. The man leaning on the railing next door might well have been Ross. Eight years was plenty of time for his unsavory San Francisco associates to forget about him. As Alison had said, he would have no fear of coming back here now.

I looked at the picture again, but by now my recollection of the man next door had become blurred. The more I tried to bring it into focus the faster it faded, until I couldn't recall a single feature clearly.

Michelle and Craig's closet was also as it had been two hours ago—jammed. Nothing had been removed. Did that mean Ross had not come for clothes but for something else? Household money perhaps? Or maybe he had had second thoughts and not come in at all. Or maybe he wasn't Ross.

I sank down on the bed. In the heat of the afternoon it was very appealing. Was there anything to do but wait for Ward McElvey to come home? And when he did, would he remember having seen the man on his porch? Would he know if he was Ross? But even if he was Ross, that didn't mean he was having an affair with Michelle.

The sensible thing to do would be to lock the house and drive home to salvage the rest of the day. I could call Vida when she got off work and tell her

. . . No. As long as it wasn't definite, I would hold off telling Vida my suspicions.

There was one more person to talk to—Father Calloway. He had dropped Michelle downtown last night. She told him she was getting out to catch up with a man she knew. Surely he had looked to see who it was. Father Calloway had been the priest at St. Agnes' for years. If Ross were Catholic he would have known him; if not, he might still have some memory of him, particularly if I could jog that memory with Ross's picture.

Holding the picture by the edges, I pulled the front door shut and hurriedly started down the stairs. What time did priests eat dinner? Five? Five-thirty? If I drove fast, I might be able to catch Father Calloway before—

I stepped on the ivy. My foot slipped. I grabbed for the railing. It was too late. Both feet were in the air. I landed hard on my bottom and bounced down to the step below.

"Damn!"

My shoulder ached; I wriggled my bottom to see if it was still in one piece. Then I felt my jeans for rips. They too were whole. But that ameliorated the situation only slightly. It wasn't till I looked up that I realized I had let go of the photo. I eyed the stairs, the ivy, and the road; I spotted it just as a breeze carried it into the sewer hole.

"Damn! Damn!" Somehow, the picture falling into the sewer hole pretty well summed up my day.

I dusted off my jeans, rubbed my bruised bottom, and walked down the steps to the hole.

Through the cracks between the boards I could see only darkness. There was nothing to do but shift the boards. I grabbed the edge of one, pulled it up, and flipped it over onto the road.

I looked back into the hole and choked off a scream.

At the bottom of the hole, next to the end of the sewer pipe, was Michelle Davidson. She lay on her back, her arms at her sides. Her brown eyes were open wide, but weren't looking. A spray of dirt had landed on her face and in her open eyes. There was no question that she was dead.

I called the Sheriff's Department from Michelle's house, then walked back outside and down the steps slowly, and sat, still shaking, as two deputies pulled up and walked to the hole. I answered the questions one of them asked.

Sheriff Wescott arrived, and then the department photographer, the ambulance, and the doctor. Neighbors began to emerge from their houses and formed a group at the far side of the street. The McElveys were not among them. I recognized only faces; I couldn't have put names to any of them.

The sheriff's contingent seemed to talk among themselves for a long time. I could hear words but I made no attempt to put them into sentences. One of the neighbors walked away and returned with a ladder, and first one of the ambulance men, and then the sheriff, climbed down into the sewer hole. The others stared over the edge.

I pushed myself up and walked toward the sewer hole. The neighbors had stayed back. None of the deputies seemed to notice me. They were all looking down.

A light covering of dirt overlaid Michelle's body, as if a mourner had thrown in a traditional handful

after the graveside service. But Michelle looked like
a parody of the traditional corpse. Her arms lay near
her sides and her legs were straight but flung apart,
as if her torso and arms had hit the damp earth in
the hole and stuck but her legs had been jerked up
by the force of her fall and came down apart. Her
long brown hair was wet and hung limply. Her face
was a sallow gray-green; it looked more like a mask
than something that had recently been alive.

The sheriff climbed back up. Another ambulance
crew member lowered the stretcher down and then
climbed in after it.

I didn't need to see Michelle's body belted onto it
and lifted out. I didn't want to see the dirt that had
been sprinkled over her face and stuck to her eyes. I
wanted to sit on the steps with a very strong drink.
Instead, I took a breath and walked up to Sheriff
Wescott. Michelle's murder was his business now. I
said, "I spent some time checking into where Michelle was last night."

As he turned to me his tanned brown face wrinkled; the corners of his mouth moved but I couldn't
tell whether he had instinctively started to smile as
he recognized me, or grimace in recollection of the
murder investigation I had been involved with in
March. There were things I hadn't told him then,
things I could never admit. He suspected that then
and it had added an edge to our encounters. He ran
a hand through his curly brown hair. "Does no one
die in this town without your attention?"

Ignoring that, I said, "Michelle had a boyfriend in
high school, a guy who was older than she was.
People speculate that she was still fascinated by him
even though he hasn't lived here in years. His name
was Ross Remson."

Out of the side of my eye I could see the ambulance crew lifting Michelle's body out of the sewer hole. I swallowed.

Wescott had turned to watch them. To me he said, "So?"

"I'm just trying to pass on what I know to make your murder investigation a little easier."

"Murder?" he said, drawing his attention back to me. "What makes you think this is murder? A woman comes home from a bar, falls into a fifteen-foot hole and hits her head on the end of a sewer pipe, and you instantly suspect murder."

I stood staring at the hole a moment. It hadn't occurred to me that he could assume otherwise. I started to protest, then caught myself. Why was it I suspected Michelle had been murdered? Was it just because I had been checking on her disappearance? Was it because I assumed she had been with Ross (Ross who lots of people viewed with suspicion)? So now I assumed Ross had killed Michelle? Was that all? Was Sheriff Wescott correct in saying that I instantly suspected murder?

But no. There was more. There was something about Michelle's body.

"You don't fall down a hole like this backwards," I said. "We're all familiar with the sewer hole. We give it a wide berth automatically, as if it were already filled with sewage. I've caught myself doing that. I've seen other people. No one strolls right next to it as if it were a pothole."

"So?" He glared down at the hole. Beyond it one of the deputies was driving off.

"So Michelle wouldn't be casually standing at the edge and step back by mistake."

"Look, you told the deputy that she came home

from a bar. You don't know what time she got here. She was probably drunk. Half the Russian River area is drunk. If we didn't have drunks driving into trees, getting into fights, falling down flights of stairs, or wading out into the river until they forget where they are and drown, we wouldn't need two-thirds of the sheriffs here."

"You don't know she was drunk."

"We'll find out. The lab will tell us." He took a step toward his car.

"When?" I demanded.

"As soon as they can," he snapped. "It's a busy time for them. It's not just the merchants who do a big business when the Bohemians are here. The lab's got plenty of samples to analyze and they'll have lots more as soon as the festivities get going proper."

"So the question of whether Michelle Davidson was murdered is going to sit on the back burner?"

"I didn't say that."

"You didn't say anything definite."

He took another step and then swiveled back to face me. "Is there something conclusive, some piece of evidence that you want to tell me about? You're good at concealing evidence, I know that. Now if there's something that's made you decide this is murder, tell me."

I had seen his face harden like this before. It had the leathery look of suntan and of disgust. His blue eyes looked icy. There might be more behind that expression, but it was impossible for me to say what it was.

"Michelle was a gymnast. She had good balance. She knew how to move. Even if she had been drink-ing she'd still have better reactions than you or I.

She wouldn't fall flat on her back like that. She would roll instinctively."

"Everyone has off days."

"Then what about the boards. The boards that covered the sewer hole were too close together for her to have fallen between them—particularly backwards."

He glanced at the hole. "One board wasn't even on it."

"I know. I moved it."

"You what?"

"Well, I needed to see down there. I wasn't looking for a body—" I caught myself before admitting I was looking for Ross's picture. "I explained all this to your deputy."

"How close were the boards then?"

I held my hands about a foot apart.

"That's what you remember now?" he asked.

"Give or take."

"Uh-huh. 'Give or take.' Six inches or twelve or fifteen. She was a small woman. She could have fallen through."

"No, she couldn't have."

He shook his head. "I have only your very inexact recollection for that. I can't base an investigation on that, not this week."

"You can't just let this go so you can have more men patrolling the streets. Michelle Davidson had a family. It will make a big difference to them whether she came home so drunk that she fell into a sewer and died, or whether she was murdered. If you leave them with that question, it's like sticking her body in their living room until you're ready to deal with it."

Under his suntan his face flushed with anger. "I said I'll handle this investigation. That's what I do.

That's why I'm a sheriff and you are a meter reader.
So leave it alone, okay?"

"Are you through with me then?" I said, matching the anger in his voice.

"I just want you to tell me that you're going to
stay out of this."

But that was the one thing I couldn't do.

I sat in the cab of my pickup and watched Sheriff
Wescott drive back toward town.

I hadn't realized till I blurted it out to the sheriff
how undignified Michelle Davidson's death was. In
life she had been the pompom leader, the prom
queen. Once it became known she died from a
drunken fall into a sewer that would be all people
would remember. If people did think beyond that
epitaph, they would add that she got that drunk
with a *man*. There would be plenty of speculation
about that.

Would this occur to the sheriff? I doubted it. Sheriff Wescott was a decent man. I knew he was competent and fair, and would do the best he could. But
even the most conscientious lawman couldn't do everything at this time of the year. He himself had said
the Sheriff's Department was wildly overworked
during Bohemian Week. Besides the drunk driving,
there were the confrontations that came when the
mighty and the servants thereof strolled into town
expecting special consideration. There might not be
many, but one or two was all the Sheriff's Department needed. When they ran afoul of the local people who were barely scratching out a living legally,
or making ends meet by forays into the not-so-legal,
there was little tolerance on either side. The Russian
River area had its share of mountain men who were

no respecters of chairmen of the board or assistants to chairmen. And there were the tourist families and gays. With the festival atmosphere in town and the river of beer that accompanied it, there was a big potential for violence. It was much too great a potential to leave the sheriff time to investigate something that looked like an accidental death.

Still, it was possible that Sheriff Wescott might come around to thinking Michelle's death was murder. But he wouldn't do that until after the lab report came back, and that might be days. By that time Ross would be gone. He would be out of town, out of state, or even out of the country.

Right now the sheriff would be heading for the nursery to tell Craig Davidson his wife was dead. What I had to do was find Ross. But first I had to see Father Calloway. For him to identify the man Michelle had met last night he would need to see Ross's picture. And that was still down in the sewer hole.

I climbed out of my truck and reluctantly walked back to the hole. I scanned the edges of it, hoping that somehow the photo had got stuck within reaching distance. It hadn't.

There was nothing to do but climb down. That meant crossing the sheriff's cordon. It also meant getting a ladder out of the garage.

I tried the garage door. Not surprisingly, it was locked. Only those who wished to let their belongings circulate left garages unlocked. But there was a window on the side by the staircase. It was open, probably to air out the smell of the cesspool runoff and the mosquito larvae. I hesitated only briefly. If I were seen crossing the sheriff's cordon and climbing into the sewer, being spotted breaking into the garage wouldn't make things much worse.

Hoisting myself through the window was no problem. Once inside, I found an extension ladder hanging on hooks on the far wall, right above the slimy patch. The garage door pushed up easily, and in a minute I was back outside.

I lowered the ladder into the hole and, without looking to see who might be watching, climbed down.

It was dark in the hole. Tomblike. My eyes adjusted slowly. It made me shiver to realize that this *had* been Michelle's tomb. It was also wetter than I had expected. Half Hill Road is partway up the hill. Even a fifteen-foot hole wouldn't be below water level. But there are springs, and the ground holds water from the winter rains. For whatever reason, the bottom of the hole was squishy with mud. Gingerly I put a foot down, still hanging onto the ladder.

The place where Michelle's body had landed, next to the end of the sewer pipe, was a mound of earth higher than the surrounding areas. On either side of the pipe was a shallow ditch. It was in one of these that I stood, now ankle-deep in mud. I turned, forcing myself to survey the near wall of the hole foot by foot, looking for the picture. But it had not stuck to that wall.

I took three careful steps, positioning myself in front of the wall opposite the end of the pipe. It was a bit better lighted and it took me less time to conclude the photo wasn't there either.

The far wall was also bare. I turned back around. The mud was cold and had splattered my jeans. I glanced at the mound of dirt, sure the picture would not still be lying on it. Had it landed there the sheriff would have spotted it and taken it out with the body.

But it had to be in this hole. I had seen it go in. Now I looked at the pipe, *in* the pipe as best I could, and beneath the sides of it. And there, stuck under the pipe, was the photo. My hands were muddy. I picked up the photo by the edges and started up the ladder, moving carefully, afraid of dropping it back into the hole.

The sunlight hit me all at once. I closed my eyes against it and felt its warmth on my cheek. Turning away from the light, I opened my eyes and climbed the rest of the way up the ladder. It wasn't till I was about to step out that I saw Craig Davidson staring down at me.

Behind him was Sheriff Wescott.

jammed the photo in my pocket, wiped my hand on my jeans, and climbed out of the sewer hole.

Before I could speak, Sheriff Wescott said, "Didn't you hear me before? Not half an hour ago? I said stay out of this case. Out! And I barely leave the street before you climb down into the one place that's off-limits."

I said nothing.

"I could book you for this. You know that, don't you?"

I nodded.

"Okay, but I expect you to tell me, honestly and without withholding as much as a thought, what you were doing down in that sewer hole."

I had no choice. "I dropped something into the hole. That's how I happened to be looking down there when I spotted Michelle's body." I glanced uncomfortably at Craig. He had moved back a few steps and was leaning against the stair railing. If he noted anything either of us said, he gave no sign of it. He merely looked dazed.

"What did you drop?" the sheriff demanded.

I extricated the snapshot of Ross and Michelle from my pocket and handed it to him, feeling like a naughty child. The photo was creased from being jammed into my pocket and was smudged with mud, but both the faces were still recognizable.

Sheriff Wescott looked down at it a moment and then, almost involuntarily, glanced at Craig. Motioning me to the far side of the hole, away from Craig, he said, "Who is this man?"

"The one I tried to tell you about, the old boy-friend."

"The one you've decided makes this a murder case, eh? So you took it upon yourself to break through our cordon, climb down into the secured area, and get it, is that it?"

"That's it," I said, involuntarily mimicking his tone. "And since it's so irrelevant to your case, I'll take it back."

"Anything in the hole is evidence."

"Evidence of what, if you don't think there was a crime?"

"Evidence."

"If I hadn't searched for that you'd have never known it was there," I said, realizing as I said it, that this line of complaint was going to get me nowhere.

Instead of giving me back Ross's picture, Wescott made me describe my search for it, where I had looked, where I'd stepped. The photo he deposited in a plastic bag.

"I want you to understand that this is the last time for anything like this. The next time you do something that is not thoroughly legal, completely above-board, you can count on being a guest of the county. Is that clear?"

"What?" Behind Ward McElvey's house a man stood looking down at us.

"I said, the next time I catch you at anything illegal, you go to jail. Understand now?"

I was sure the man was Ross Remson. Or almost sure. It was that flicker of doubt that kept me from pointing him out to the sheriff. Then he turned and walked behind Ward's house.

"Is that all?" I said to the sheriff.

"It had better be."

I forced myself to walk, not run, around the sewer hole and down the street past Ward's house. With each step my pace quickened. On the far side of Ward's was an older house, the one with the yard Ward crossed. I looked between the houses, but there was no sight of Ross. I hurried on till I could see between the next two houses. Nothing moved. Ross had been walking too. How had I missed him? Maybe he had started running as soon as he was out of view of the sheriff. I rushed down past the next house, but again there was no running man, no branches waving in the still afternoon.

If these houses were like mine there would be a path behind them that led to a commonly used spring. It would be easy for Ross to lope along that but not to run all out. I couldn't believe he had outdistanced me and still left no trace of his flight.

But if he hadn't run beyond this spot where was he? Had he hidden somewhere along the path? Was he lurking behind an outbuilding waiting to hear the sheriff's car leave? It might be a long wait. Even then he would have to get down without being spotted. He had grown up here. People would recognize him. They wouldn't think of him as a murderer, but they would find it noteworthy that he had returned to Henderson after being gone so long.

Of course, he was familiar with the terrain. For someone who knew the area the sensible thing to do would be to go uphill, to come out on Cemetery Road, the street above, and stroll back to his car. And the most likely place to park without drawing notice would be at the old Henderson cemetery at the top of the hill. The graves there were old. Relatives of the entombed had long since died and been buried in the new cemetery across the river. Now the only people who visited the cemetery were those who for one reason or another wanted the solitude.

I walked quickly up Half Hill Road. My pickup was on the near side of the sewer hole. The sheriff's car was next to it, but fortunately the sheriff himself was nowhere in sight. He must have gone into Craig's house.

I climbed into the cab of my pickup, backed into a driveway, and turned toward town.

I took a right on Zeus Lane, up the hill toward Cemetery Road. I barely had time to slam on the brakes. A Winnebago blocked the street. Its nose was in a driveway.

"Could you pull in?" I hollered to the driver.

He looked confused. "Waiting for the wife," he called. "Never can finish her good-byes in less than an hour. You'd think she—"

"I need to get by," I yelled. "I'm in a hurry."

"Oh. Sure." He started the engine and inched the huge vehicle into the driveway.

I raced by and cut left onto Cemetery Road.

Cemetery Road paralleled Half Hill Road then cut sharply uphill to wind its way past a few dead-end streets before it reached the cemetery itself. It was possible that Ross could have driven into one of those dead ends but unlikely since he had no reason to think anyone was looking for him. If he didn't, and if he hadn't followed Cemetery Road down across Zeus Lane and into town at the other end of the shopping area, then he was somewhere on this street. Or in the cemetery itself.

Cemetery Road was narrower than Half Hill. Beside it the ground rose or dropped steeply. The houses were newer, had large decks, and looked precarious. The only vehicle parked on the street was a county car and it was empty. I drove slowly, checking as best I could for a tall sandy-haired man who might be hiding behind a eucalyptus tree or making his way up the street. But when I reached the cemetery I still hadn't seen him.

The entrance to the cemetery was marked by cement pillars between which a gate may once have hung. If so, it had been stolen long ago. Now even the pillars were worn, like the teeth of an old dog. I drove along the dirt road. Clumps of stone suggested it had been covered with gravel at a time when that was as close to paving as any road in this area got. But that time was long ago. Now the road was dusty and deeply pitted and even in a pickup the going was rough.

I drove on to a flat spot at the top of the hill—the parking area. There was no other vehicle here.

Briefly I considered racing back down into town to see if Ross was there. But he wouldn't be. That would be crazy. He wouldn't rush away from Michelle's house so fast that I couldn't find any remnant of his being there just to be seen on North Bank Road.

I got out of my truck and walked toward the gravestones as I had done on many occasions when I wanted to think. After the sepulchral sewer hole the shady cemetery seemed almost cheerful. It bore no resemblance to newer memorial parks where unobtrusive memorial plaques are camouflaged so they won't mar the landscaping. Worn, cracked, their lettering so faint as to no longer reveal who rested beneath, the gravestones here were grouped in family plots. Tarnished low brass rails enclosed the ten-by-twenty-foot rectangles.

The mud from the sewer hole still caked my feet; leaves stuck to the mud; and my feet seemed part of the earth beneath. I felt a surprisingly easy affinity with the other inhabitants here. A cool dusk breeze lifted the leaves and passed like a shawl over my arms. It was nice to be here in the silence, with no awkward questions to ask, no sheriff to threaten me. I sat down on a long flat stone, picked up a dead pine branch, and began half-heartedly dusting the mud from my jeans.

The man I had followed had eluded me. But suppose that man wasn't Ross. I had only my own assumption to say that he was. It was reasonable to assume that a man who merely looked like Ross might have been walking down the street—but standing in Ward's backyard? What was he doing there if he wasn't Ross?

Assuming he was Ross, why would he have left Henderson so suddenly as to miss his father's funeral, and then return eight years later to kill a girl he had dated when she was in high school? Was there more to it than that? Alison Barluska hadn't mentioned any letters or phone calls from Michelle when she was living with Ross. But Ross might have kept in contact. Alison, as she had said, wasn't the love of Ross's life. His living with her wouldn't have precluded visits to Michelle. Perhaps he had come to Henderson when Craig was away. Perhaps Michelle had told Craig she was going to visit her sister in Santa Rosa and gone on to San Francisco to meet Ross. But even if that were so, even if they had carried on a clandestine romance all these years, why would Ross have killed her now?

The branch cracked halfway. I tore the end loose and continued to brush.

According to Ward, Michelle hadn't had enough to do now that her children were in school. Craig spent long hours at the plant nursery. Michelle was irritated about Alison working there. Was this then the time that Michelle had decided to run off with Ross? Had Ross objected (was it more than he had in mind?), Michelle insisted, and he killed her? Wait —rather than kill her, wouldn't it have been easier for Ross just to stay out of Henderson?

It would, unless Michelle had had some hold on him. Suppose she had known he was the Bohemian Connection. He had told Alison; maybe he also bragged to Michelle. Whatever he did as the Bohemian Connection included the illegal.

But it had been eight years since he had been the Connection. Unless he was involved in something more felonious than Alison had intimated, the statute of limitations would have run out on any crime he had committed.

I pushed myself up and strolled along the overgrown path between the families of gravestones. The path was thick with pine needles, so that even the sound of my steps was muffled. I felt like I was walking on pillows. A redwood tree, older than any of the dead beneath the ground, shaded the nearer plots. In winter it would shield them from the driving rain. Now its shade was dark against the patches of bright setting sun. I walked to the farthest plot, that of Maria Keneally and her five children, all of whom had died before the age of ten. She had outlived the last of them by thirty years. When I worked the hillside route the cemetery was a good place for lunch. I had sat here many times before when I wanted to sort things out. I had wondered about Maria Keneally and her sad life.

I sat again on her stone and stared beyond the cemetery at a log house thirty yards away. The house was owned by her niece, an old woman of the same name. When I came to read her meter, she always rushed out, offered me tea (an offer no one who works outside all day can afford to accept), and invariably stated that it was good for an old lady to live so close to the cemetery. Not so far to go.

After the initial shock, I had smiled at the old refrain. I hadn't mentioned that this old cemetery was full and her remains would have to be taken to the new graveyard across the river.

As it turned out, she went to neither, but in May had gone for a summerlong visit to a niece, yet another Maria Keneally, in County Cork. Her yard, however, was so clearly untended that it looked as if she had been deposited in the graveyard.

A squirrel ran across the yard in front of the house and toward the giant redwood.

Enough of houses and rodents, I told myself. Why would Ross have killed Michelle? Even though Ross hadn't been the Bohemian Connection for eight years, the need he had filled in that job still existed. Men still had rendezvous, doubtless still coveted a lid of grass or a snort of coke. So if Ross were no longer the Bohemian Connection, who was? Craig? Ward? Or some other man?

Or did the Connection have to be a man? A chairman of the board might be unnerved to discover his illicit rendezvous was arranged by a woman, but his minions wouldn't care. And marijuana farmers and coke dealers will sell to anyone. No, there was no reason the Bohemian Connection couldn't be a woman.

Ross had had the necessary contacts both at the Grove and in town. Whoever had taken over after him needed to know those people. The locals would deal only with someone they could trust, and the visitors would be even warier. The only way both groups could feel sure of the new Connection would be if that person were Ross's hand-picked successor.

Besides having Ross's trust, what would someone need in order to be the Connection? A working relationship with the local suppliers. A good knowledge of the area. No one who wandered in cold from San Francisco or Oakland could find a suitable rendezvous for a company president and his lover and know where to get good grass from the backwoods gardens to the north of here. And the Connection would need his time to be flexible. A sudden rush of demands couldn't be handled in half an hour. It was hardly work that could be farmed out.

Of the people I had met asking about Michelle's disappearance, it was Michelle herself who most nearly fit this description. Michelle had had more time than she could handle. She had grown up in Henderson, gone to school here, known all the winter people. And perhaps more importantly, she alone had trusted Ross. It was she whom he could trust in return. It was she to whom he could turn over the Connection trade knowing it would stay as he had left it.

Or could he? Eight years can alter a lot. In less time than that every cell in the body changes. In those eight years the Michelle who had been an adoring high school girl had become a woman. In that time the Bohemian Connection might no longer have been Ross's gift to her, but have become her own business. That didn't seem like something Ross would comprehend easily.

Had Ross come back wanting a share of his trade? Or perhaps all of it? Had he viewed the intervening years as a period when Michelle ran a business for him, just marking time till he returned and took charge again? Had he announced as much and Michelle objected? Had they had a few drinks, walked back to Michelle's house, argued, and he killed her?

Leaves crackled. I looked toward the empty house. The screen door was open and by it stood Alison Barluska.

"Maria Keneally's not home, Alison," I called.

Alison turned abruptly. I couldn't make out her expression at that distance. From her movements she seemed startled.

I stood up and called to her again. Alison was just the person I needed to see. She could tell me if Ross had received letters from Michelle. I hadn't asked her specifically. And she could tell me in greater detail—much greater detail—what Ross had done as the Bohemian Connection. I glanced down, looking for the path through the underbrush. When I looked up Alison was hurrying around the side of the house toward the driveway.

"Alison, wait!" I called.

She disappeared behind the house and in a minute I heard her truck pull away.

I hurried across to the house. Vines grew up the wood sides. The yard was a scramble of low weeds and pine needles. There was another old redwood at the edge of the property that shaded the yard and allowed it to survive untended without being totally overgrown.

Before she left, Maria Keneally had told me she would unplug all her electric appliances. I had asked her if she wouldn't feel safer leaving a light on a timer. Housebreaking was an ongoing business in the river area. Each winter, after the summer people had left, a changing crew of winter residents began breaking in. Anyone who went off in September leaving a television or stereo should have been surprised to find it still there when he came back in June. The occasional house was guarded by alarms, a few even connected to the sheriff's department. But alarms were impractical, particularly for houses as isolated as this one.

Maria Keneally had been pleased at my concern. She'd made a point of taking me into her living room and showing me her father's antique pistol that she kept by the door to her garage. "Still shoots 'em dead," she'd assured me. She wasn't about to let any shiftless layabout from Guerneville or Monte Rio break into her house and steal her television when she was there, nor did she intend to pay the electric company for light when she wasn't. And that was that.

I checked the windows now. No wires were visible. But I hardly expected Maria Keneally to have paid for an alarm system. So it would have been easy for anyone to break a windowpane and let himself in.

I walked around the house till I found the broken window, a bathroom window shielded from view by overgrown bushes.

Had Alison broken in here? I had only seen her at

the door. Had she been canvassing and knocked, waited, and was leaving when I spotted her?

I hurried down to the end of the driveway. The Davidson's Plants truck was not parked by any of the other houses down the road. Alison wasn't knocking at doors there.

So, if not canvassing, what had Alison been doing here?

CHAPTER
7

I drove by Davidson's Plants, prepared to ask Alison Barluska what she had been doing at old Miss Keneally's house. But the nursery was closed and the nursery truck was not in the lot. So Alison had not come back here.

No matter what Alison had been doing there, I felt sure she would tell me she was canvassing. She might have been working with Ross and checking out the isolated house to use for rendezvous. But she wouldn't tell me that. She'd say she was canvassing for the gardening service. Or, indeed, she *might* have been canvassing.

Ross had been the Bohemian Connection. Had he been succeeded by Michelle, or Alison? Or had all three of them been in it together? Or . . .

Before I tried to make sense of that I needed to be sure the man Michelle had met downtown last night *was* Ross. For that I had to talk to Father Calloway.

St. Agnes' Roman Catholic Church was nearly halfway to the Pacific Ocean. St. Elizabeth's in Guerneville was closer to Henderson, but most of the fishing families had been parishioners of St. Agnes' for generations. It was Father Calloway who blessed the fishing fleet. It was there that potluck dinners were organized to welcome the men back from the sea. And while the Ricollos and the Luccis,

Michelle's father's family, no longer fished, St. Agnes' was still their spiritual home.

Near the church the land flattened, beginning the transition from the steep tree- and fern-covered hills, which were so much a part of the Russian River area, to Pacific beachfront. Here the redwoods and eucalyptus grew farther back from the road. The underbrush thinned, replaced by grassy mounds. Small flocks of sheep grazed.

It was on one of these mounds that St. Agnes' sat, its dark green wood unprotected from the strong ocean winds. A small plain church, it had been built when the living Maria Keneally was a girl. Climbing roses covered the west side, and a low garden of seasonal flowers was on the east. Behind the rectory was a vegetable plot, and it was there that I usually encountered Father Calloway while out on my route. In baggy corduroys and an old chamois shirt, both well coated with dirt, he was usually bending over bare soil. There was never a pea or bean in that garden. Either it was too early and he was just preparing the soil, or he had planted but nothing had come up yet, or the seedlings had broken the ground and the deer and groundhogs had eaten them. His gift to the less fortunate, he called it.

It was after seven o'clock as I pulled into the empty parking lot. I walked around the east side of the church, past the heat-wilted plants, to the rectory, knocked, and waited.

After a moment a middle-aged woman in an apron opened the door.

"I'm here to see Father Calloway," I said.

"He's gone off," she said with a reinforcing nod of the head. "To see that poor family, you know."

"When was that?"

"Five-thirty."

"Do you expect him back soon then?"

"I'm sure I wouldn't know. I'm just leaving, myself. I'm only a daily. Father Calloway doesn't have a real housekeeper anymore, you see." Her tone suggested that Father Calloway had come down in the world.

"I'll wait."

"As you wish. You can sit in his study, through here." She stepped back and indicated a rather dark room on the left. "Tell him I left a casserole in the oven. All he needs to do is turn it on. Three hundred fifty degrees for an hour, tell him."

"I will."

She pulled the study door shut after her and in a moment I saw her clumping through the parking lot, her apron still in place like a uniform. There had been no car in the lot. Briefly I wondered how she got home.

The study had the obligatory bookcases and a desk by the window with a pair of wooden chairs facing it. The desk chair itself was padded and looked like a seat in which a priest could conjure uplifting thoughts hour after hour. Presumably, parishioners who had need to consult their priest were so unlikely to be comfortable that there was no sense wasting money padding *their* chairs. To the side of the desk on the west wall was a stone fireplace large enough to warm the room on the coldest day. Now the dark room was refreshingly cool.

I eyed the bookshelves but they held only ecclesiastical books, and in any case I was hardly in the frame of mind to read. I was just about to sit on one of the hard chairs when the study door opened.

Father Calloway was a small portly man with a

round ruddy face, gray eyes, and thick white hair. No feature stood out, and there was something rather comforting about that. His was a face you could tell your problems to without dreading any sharp rejoinder. His black suit seemed oddly formal on him. And the smile that came so easily in his garden was an effort now.

"Vejay Haskell," I said, extending a hand. "I'm your meter reader. But I'm not here on business, mine or yours," I added almost automatically. "I want to ask you something. Oh, and your house-keeper told me that she left a casserole in the oven for you."

"Ah, I'm sure she did."

"I'll wait while you put the oven on," I said, sitting down.

Instead of heading for the kitchen, he settled in his chair. "Perhaps later. I can't say I feel much like eating." Sitting there with the evening light coming through the window behind him, he looked very weary.

"Michelle Davidson? Was it her family you were going to see?"

"Yes. Poor girl. Two small children, too."

"I guess you knew her pretty well."

"I did at that. Since she was a child. I've been the priest here for nearly twenty years. Lovely family the Riccolos. I knew Michelle's mother, God rest her soul, and her aunt, Vida, and her boys. Michelle never missed a Sunday."

"That's unusual these days."

"It is at that."

It must be hard for him to comfort Craig and Vida and absorb his own grief, too, I thought. And my questions weren't going to make this day any more pleasant for him. "It's Michelle I came to ask about," I said. "She was involved in the anti-prostitution group, wasn't she?"

"She was. But why are you asking this when the poor girl's not even in the ground?"

"I don't think she stumbled into that sewer hole and died. She didn't die because she was too drunk to walk straight. There's more to it than that."

He sat forward, his finger poised on the desk.

"Vida asked me to look into it."

He nodded noncommittally.

"You were one of the last persons to see Michelle alive."

He sank back. It was clear that, like Vida, he felt responsible for Michelle's being downtown, where danger could overcome her.

"Tell me about this anti-prostitution group," I said.

He sighed. "Michelle organized it. She asked me to help with it. Of course, I am expected to do what I can to stop that type of thing."

"How many are in the group?"

"Let me see—Mrs. Perkins, Mrs. Bender, Mrs. O'Leary, um, um . . . Maybe eight or nine."

"What possessed Michelle to start it?"

He sighed again. "To tell you the truth, I don't know. She said the prostitutes walking around town with all their ill-gotten cash were a bad influence on the children. There's no denying that. They do give the impression that prostitution is a glamorous way of life. A fancy blond in hot pants flaunting hundred-dollar bills looks much more appealing to a teenage girl than her mother standing over the sink. But to answer your question, I don't know if that was the total reason or not."

"Eight people doesn't seem like enough for a demonstration to be taken seriously."

"Well, normally you would be right, but in this case it wouldn't have mattered. There'll be plenty of other demonstrators outside the Grove—anti-nuclear people, anti-military, environmentalists, those opposing contracts with South Africa, and so on. We would have been just one more group blending in. When the television reporters interviewed Michelle . . . well, they won't be doing that, will they?"

I waited a moment. "Did you know Ross Remson?"

"A bad one, that boy," he said without pause for thought. As soon as the words were out he looked regretful.

"Not one of your congregation then?"

"Yes and no. The boy was baptized here. Before my time that was. His sister the year after. But they never came to Mass, none of them, the children or the mother. And the father wasn't of the faith."

"It's odd they were baptized, then."

"Not so uncommon as you might think. A mother feels guilty when she's married outside the Church, particularly to a man like Leo Remson." Seeing my questioning look, he said, "Leo played around and drank in the early years. Eventually he pulled himself together, but by then it was too late for his missus. Her nerves were never strong. Too much responsibility. But she did get the children baptized. She exerted her will those two times. Perhaps it was all she could do. Perhaps she hoped baptism would protect the children, like inoculations."

"It doesn't sound like it did."

"Maybe some day. The ways of the Lord . . ."

His voice trailed off. "But the girl went off to college and came back with a husband much like her father. And Ross, well, he was wild."

"You did see them then?"

"The girl I don't think I ever spoke to, but Ross came to some of the Saturday night dances here. We have them in the winter. I think the girl felt awkward coming here to dance and not to Mass. But the boy, Ross, he had no sense of shame. He walked through the door like he had been here every Sunday, came up and greeted me by name, just as if he knew me. Of course, I didn't say anything. You don't get them in here by reminding them they've been remiss."

"Is this where he met Michelle?"

"Oh, I'd hate to think we were responsible." Again he looked appalled that the deprecatory thought had slipped out.

"Was he a bad influence on her?" I asked, curious to see how widely known Ross's effect on Michelle was.

He hesitated. "I suppose since I've said that much I should make my thoughts clear."

I waited.

"He was. Always wild, that boy. Always on the edge of trouble, always able to keep from slipping over even if those who were with him weren't so skillful. There were a number of car thefts and joy rides that were never solved when Ross was in high school. He was doing them, but there was never the proof to arrest him."

That would fit with the Ross who had moved to San Francisco and found "friends" so menacing that he'd decided to disappear from sight. I said, "I understand Ross was what was called 'the Bohemian

Connection.' That seems a bit out of your purview, but I rather hoped you might be able to tell me about that." The question was a long shot. I didn't know whether Father Calloway would even recognize the term "Bohemian Connection."

"You'd be surprised what I do know," Father Calloway said. "It's not that people tell me, at least not that they intend to enlighten me. But they do mention parts of stories, and they talk among themselves when I'm nearby. And the children, of course, repeat anything. I have a lot of time to fit the parts together. You learn to do that when you're called upon to counsel people. It gets easier, maybe too easy. Concern becomes curiosity, even nosiness."

"So you do know about the Bohemian Connection?"

"Its existence is no secret, or maybe it's more accurate to say it's a very poorly kept secret. There's always been a Connection. Before Ross, I don't know who did it. The identity usually has been hidden."

"Who inherited the job from Ross?"

"Now that I don't know."

"Michelle?"

"Oh no. She was a lovely girl. She had a good life, a fine husband, two beautiful children. Everything she wanted. She would never have thought of anything like that."

Suddenly the limitations of this man struck me. Was he constrained by his doctrine to believe that marriage and motherhood had to be enough? Was he unaware that Michelle Davidson looked for causes to give some meaning to her life?

"You drove Michelle back from the meeting last

night. You let her off downtown. How did that happen?"

"We were talking about, let me see, ah, yes, the altar flowers. The altar guild should be taking care of them but in the summer they do get a bit forgetful. Michelle mentioned that last Sunday's flowers were looking limp. And then, in the middle of her sentence, she said, 'Let me out!' Just like that."

"Is that all she said?"

"It is, almost. She said, 'There's . . .' as if she were going to name someone. Then she just said, 'Let me off here.' "

"But you said she got off to meet a *man*. How do you know it was a man?"

"I saw them walk into the bar."

"Was that man Ross Remson?" I could feel myself holding my breath.

"I never thought about Ross."

"But you did see the man?"

"Only as he was turning to go inside the bar. But, yes, it could have been Ross Remson. He was the same size; he had the same color hair. Indeed it could have been. I just never thought of Ross. He's been gone so many years. But, indeed, it could have been."

"You knew Ross. Would you think it was possible for him to push Michelle into the sewer hole hard enough to kill her?"

He stared, shocked. It was a moment before he said, "I haven't seen Ross Remson in years. I can hardly make such a damning statement."

"But if they'd both had enough to drink, argued, and then he shoved her hard and she fell, would you be surprised to discover that he had left her there?"

"Sad to say, no, I wouldn't be surprised."

It was after seven o'clock. Vida would be at Craig's house. She would think Michelle's death was due to a drunken fall. She would blame herself for not driving Michelle to her door.

I drove back quickly toward Henderson on River Road. Once in Henderson, River Road became North Bank Road. Outside the town limits it reverted to River Road. There had been debates over the years on whether Henderson should change the name of North Bank Road to conform to the area. But conformity was never popular here, and North Bank Road survived.

In winter not a week went by without reports of speeders or drunks smashing into trees along River Road, but now it was impossible to shift out of second gear. The redwood, eucalyptus, and acacia branches made a canopy over the road. I drove ridiculously close to the station wagon ahead of me, somehow assuming that getting to Vida a second or two earlier would make a difference.

When I arrived at the Davidsons' house half an hour later, Vida answered the door. Behind her I could see Craig slumped in one of the director's chairs. She started to speak, then burst into tears.

"It's not your fault, Vida," I said. "Really it isn't."

She stepped back, still sobbing. "If I'd picked her up . . ."

"It's not your fault. I'll explain."

"I was annoyed with her. That was it. I couldn't admit it. If I'd been honest, maybe—"

"Vida, nothing you could have done would have changed what happened. You could have driven her to her doorstep and she would still be dead now."

She wiped her eyes and stared at me.

"Father Calloway dropped her downtown because she saw a man she knew. That man was probably Ross Remson."

"Ross!"

"Yes. I saw him here this morning, behind Ward's house. And he was here this afternoon after Michelle's body was taken away. He was behind the house. I tried to follow him but I lost him. Father Calloway thinks the man downtown was Ross."

"But after all this time, why would Ross come back?"

"That I don't know. But you do realize, don't you, Vida, that if Michelle saw Ross, nothing would have kept her from going downtown after him. It wouldn't have mattered whether Father Calloway dropped her there or you brought her home. She would have walked downtown after you left."

"But she might not have seen him."

"Maybe not then. Maybe later. But she would have heard he was in town. If he didn't contact her, she would have found him. Isn't that right?"

Vida didn't respond immediately, but when she did it was with a nod. Then she sobbed again, wiping the tears away as fast as they came. "Oh, Vejay, I'm so relieved. It's been awful. You just don't know. I felt so bad. I shouldn't feel better now, I know, but I do."

We stood there a moment, still at the door, before Vida motioned me in and to the empty director's chair. Craig had been close enough to hear our conversation, but if any of it registered he gave no indication. He slumped forward in the chair, staring at the floor. He looked like the African violet the man in the filthy workshirt had been buying from him this afternoon.

"Craig," I said, "I'm sorry."

"Um." He didn't look up. He seemed so deadened to emotion that I doubted much of anything would elicit a reaction from him.

Vida sat on her heels on the rug facing us. She adjusted the toes of one foot then the other. To deal with sorrow and anxiety Vida needed to be cleaning a cupboard, scrubbing a floor, or walking the steepest PG&E route in Henderson. Sitting in one place offered her no escape.

"The reason I came here when I knew you'd both be so upset is that I don't believe Michelle's death was an accident," I said.

In one move Vida stood up. Craig lifted his head.

I continued. "I think Michelle was hit on the head and then thrown into the sewer hole. I don't think she was just so drunk she stumbled in. A woman who could walk backwards on her deck railing wouldn't just fall flat on her back. Her balance was too good."

Vida nodded. "She was state champion on the balance beam. And Vejay, Michelle knew how to fall. She knew to pull her knees in and roll."

"The sheriff doesn't agree that Michelle was murdered," I said. "He doesn't disagree, but he's waiting till the medical reports are in—a couple of days probably—before he commits any manpower to this."

"Well, maybe that's sensible," Craig said. His words were sluggish.

"Days!" Vida paced in short deliberate steps from the fireplace to the wall. "In days, the murderer could be gone, the sewer hole will be filled in, and every clue will be trampled. What does the sheriff have to do that's more important than finding out who killed Michelle? Who does he think pays his salary? If he isn't here to protect the residents—"

"I agree with you," I said, relieved that Vida's and probably Craig's attention was on the murderer rather than wondering how Michelle must have felt —angry? terrified?—as she was struck on the head. "But the sheriff's really pressed right now. No matter what we think, there's no real proof Michelle was murdered. The sheriff's not going to do anything now."

"But you will, won't you, Vejay?" she demanded.

"If you want me to." I looked from Vida to Craig. He had returned to staring at the floor. "Craig?"

For a few moments he didn't speak. Then he said, "I don't know. Michelle's dead. Dead is dead. I have the children to think of. I don't want them to be in more turmoil than they have to be."

"Do you want them to hear from their friends that their mother staggered drunk into a sewer?"

His no was almost inaudible.

"Either she was murdered or she was too drunk to avoid a sewer hole she was well aware was there."

Craig stared at me, his face unnaturally pale.

"I don't mean to be crass," I said, "but time is important. Some of what I'm telling you is specula-

tion, but I'm sure that Michelle's death was no accident." I was surprised how strong my conviction
was. But then, I had seen her body lying in that hole;
I wouldn't forget that soon. "You did ask me to
investigate."

Craig was still facing me, but he seemed to be
looking through me. Again he spoke slowly. "All
right. What is it you want me to do?"

"I feel I should have your consent before I do
anything else."

"You do," Vida said before Craig could open his
mouth. He merely nodded.

"Then I'd like to ask you some questions."

"Go ahead," Vida said.

"Tell me about Thursday night, Craig."

"Well," he said, "I don't know what you want to
know. It was no different from any other Thursday
I'm at the shop. Thursdays we work late. The nursery's open till eight and then there are the week's
books to total—there's never time on Fridays because we're open later—and there are the plants to
lay out for morning and plants to replace. A customer will pick up a six-pack of delphiniums,
change his mind, and plop it down in the African
violets. So we have to check each flat of plants. And
there's sweeping up, and then the night deposit to
make."

"Who works late?"

"Both Alison and me."

"Do you go out for a beer afterwards? That
would be the normal thing to do."

"No time. The books and things take a while. If
she thinks about it early enough, sometimes Alison
goes to Thompson's Grocery and brings back beer
and sandwiches and we have them while we work."

"So how late are you there usually?"

"Why are you asking me this? You're not think-ing—"

"She's looking for a pattern, Craig," Vida said. "She figures if you're never home till twelve, anyone who wanted to would know that, right, Vejay?"

"Yes. So Craig, what time do you usually get home on Thursdays and what time did you come home last night?"

"Normally," he said, "eleven or so. Last night maybe it was a little later, maybe eleven-thirty. The books didn't balance and we had to go back over them again. I like to get home not too long after Michelle gets back."

That could have been because Michelle didn't like being alone. But I asked, "How did Michelle feel about you working late with Alison? How did she feel about Alison altogether?"

Again he hesitated. "Okay. She liked Alison okay."

"Craig," Vida said, "we've got to be straight with Vejay. We can't be asking her to investigate Mi-chelle's death and then not tell her how things are, right?" She didn't wait for a reply, but said to me, "Michelle resented Alison, right, Craig? I don't think it had much to do with Alison herself. I don't think they met more than a couple of times. Mi-chelle would have resented any woman working there."

"And the money," Craig added.

"Alison's salary?" I asked.

"Yes. Michelle seemed to think that I was *giving* Alison the money, money Michelle would rather have spent on clothes. To be honest, we had a few go-arounds about it. I tried to tell her that Alison is starting to carry her own weight. She's really getting the gardening service established. It's beginning to cover her salary. Even without that, just the publicity her canvassing brings us is worth a lot."

I questioned the need for publicity: Davidson's was the only nursery in town. But I asked, "How did Alison happen to apply at your shop?"

"She wanted nursery work. Where else would she apply?"

"Anywhere between here and Santa Cruz. She didn't have to work in Henderson."

"Well . . ."

"Craig!" Vida exclaimed.

"Well, actually, Alison knew me from the flower market," Craig said. "She was working for a florist in San Rafael, and I met her at the market a couple of times when we were both early. That was eight or nine months ago." He seemed to recognize my confusion, because he went on. "The flower market is south of San Francisco. All the growers bring in fresh flowers each morning. It opens at two A.M., or whenever the first grower arrives."

"You drive two hours or more to get there every morning at that hour?" I asked, amazed.

"No, no. We have an arrangement among some of the owners in the area. It's best if you can go yourself and choose what you want, but at that distance it's impossible. We all know generally what everyone needs. The guy who drives gets the best, but that's only fair. And it's worth it to only have to go once a week."

"Last night wasn't one of those nights, was it?"

"No. My turn is Monday morning."

"So for all intents and purposes you're gone all night every Sunday. And if anyone . . ."

"Well, no. I tried that but it just wiped me out for most of the week after. I couldn't be up all night and then be pleasant to customers all day too."

"Then you don't go?" I asked, more confused.

"Well—"

"Jenny McElvey does," Vida said. "Being an artist, she's good at choosing the flowers, right, Craig? She can use the money. And she doesn't have to deal with customers at nine in the morning."

I said, "This week she—"

"I know it's a strain on her during Bohemian Week," Craig said. "I know she'd rather not do it this week, but if she sets up her easel at one o'clock instead of noon no one cares. If she takes a break customers will come back. It's okay for artists to do things like that. It's not like owning a shop."

"Why doesn't Alison go to the flower market?"

Craig shrugged. "She didn't want to. She had to go too often in her last job. And Jenny was already going. There was no reason to change."

If Alison were the present Bohemian Connection, I could see why she wouldn't want to take the time to drive to South San Francisco. "So you met Alison at the flower market when she *did* go there. Did she say she wanted to work for you then?"

"Not the first time we met. Probably a month or so after that. It's been a good arrangement for me."

"Couldn't Michelle have canvassed or worked at the nursery?"

His face reddened. "No! I mean she could have worked in the store years ago. But then we had the children and it was reasonable that she should stay at home with them, and she didn't want to work then anyway. We never thought of the gardening service until Alison started and then I couldn't just tell Alison that it was nice that she had created this new side to the business but now I wanted my wife to do it. And besides, Michelle didn't know about gardening and Alison did."

"Do you know that log house by the cemetery?" I asked. "An old lady named Maria Keneally owns it. Does Alison garden there?"

Craig stood up. "Look, I told you the gardening is Alison's thing. I don't remember where—which houses—she goes to."

I knew I was pushing Craig to the limits of his well-controlled anger, but I went on. "Today isn't her day for canvassing, is it?"

"No. I don't know. It's her time. I don't stand over her."

"But you'd know—"

The doorbell rang. Before even Vida could get to the door Craig was there. He opened it to Sheriff Wescott.

CHAPTER
9

Sheriff Wescott greeted Vida, gave me a resigned shake of the head, and took Craig into the kitchen to talk.

"I wonder," I said to Vida, "if the sheriff has something private to discuss with Craig or if he's just annoyed to find me here."

"I could go in and see," she said.

"Can you find out later what the sheriff said and let me know, if it's important? You seem to have a good working relationship with Craig."

She laughed. It seemed like a long time since I had seen her laugh or even smile.

"You mean," she said, "that it looks like I boss Craig around. Don't let that fool you. People say Craig is a nice guy, and he is. Everyone likes Craig. Craig can be pleasant to the most irritating people. But he has his defenses too, like you saw. He'll put up with a lot before he makes a move. He's not like us, Michelle and me. We get mad and scream. Craig doesn't say anything. He hates conflict. So he takes it and takes it, and then suddenly he explodes over something so minor that it's hardly worth a grunt. Acquaintances don't see that. His customers don't. They just think he's very easygoing. He and Michelle had been married over a year before I was aware he had a temper." She glanced toward the kitchen. A low hum of male voices came from in there. "I'm not putting Craig down. I'm just saying that what's visible is not the whole picture."

I knew my time alone with Vida was limited; I couldn't ask her all the questions I needed answered. Starting at the top, I said, "You knew Michelle better than anyone. Tell me about her and Ross."

She sat on the edge of her chair, her hands moving together and apart as if to corral her thoughts. "Ross was one of those boys who was bound to end up in trouble. He flirted with trouble all through school. It was amazing enough that he managed to graduate, but that was Ross. He always survived." She leaned back. "I suppose, considering his family, he didn't have much of a chance. You know about Leo Remson, don't you?"

"That he drank and played around, you mean?"

"Yes. If Mrs. Remson had had any sense she would have thrown him out when the children were tiny. But who am I to talk? It's hard to make a decision like that when you've never worked and you have small children. There were no day-care centers in those days. Anyway, she didn't. She just suffered along. She was pretty unstable and who knows whether his behavior pushed her over the edge, or if her mental state was so rocky that she encouraged conflict. It's like an osmotic balance: when there's a lot of pressure inside it's more comfortable if there's pressure outside, too."

"Was she actually hospitalized?"

"I'm not sure. There were rumors of it, but being sent to a mental institution isn't something a person or their family talks about. Even if she wasn't committed, she was definitely unhinged. There were days when you'd see her hanging the same clothes on the line time after time—hanging them up, taking them down, and bringing them back in the house. Then half an hour later she'd hang them back up. It was sad."

"What eventually happened?"

"She drowned. Almost certainly suicide. She'd been in a bad way all summer. One August night she walked into the river. In the morning a man—thank God not a child—found her body stuck underwater on one of the summer dams by the beach. Ross was in high school then."

"There was no question that she did it herself?"

"No." Vida sighed. "But after the shock wore off and the guilt eased, it must have been a relief for the family. They could lead nearly normal lives then."

"But Ross didn't stay in Henderson," I said.

"No. It was really too late for him here. He was almost a man then. At first he'd go away for months. Then he'd come back a while and work for his father in the realty company that Ward runs now. But that arrangement was doomed. You should never let grown children come back, Vejay, believe me. You think they're still kids and they think they're James Bond." She smiled knowingly. "Leo Remson wasn't the easiest man to get along with, but he thought the world of Ross. Maybe he was trying to make up to Ross for their miserable family life. But in his eyes Ross could do no wrong. That feeling wasn't mutual. The work was too boring for Ross. He wanted excitement. One day he took off and didn't show up again until the day his father died."

"You don't think—?"

"That Ross killed his father?" Vida said. "No, it wasn't that bad a relationship, and besides, Ross hadn't been here for a year, and he'd shown a real dislike of the things he would inherit—the business and the house."

"I notice that you're not saying Ross wouldn't have done something like killing his father."

Vida tapped a finger on the arm of the chair. "No, I'm not. I'm not saying Ross would have, either. He felt that the rules set down for the average person didn't apply to him."

"Above the law?"

"Or outside its realm. And that, Vejay, was his charm, particularly for Michelle. She wanted more than just being a former pompom leader in a little town. When she won the balance beam competition, she had visions of being a star, going all the way to the Olympics. But," Vida sighed, "she was Italian."

"So?"

"You've got to be flat to be a gymnast. You've got to be shaped like a little girl, not like Michelle. Right after that competition she started to develop. You've seen her picture."

"She had a great figure." I remembered Ward McElvey commenting on that figure.

"It was great for everything but gymnastics. And what that left Michelle with was a lot of hopes and no way to fulfill them. When Ross came along, he symbolized breaking out, getting even with the rules, with the laws."

"You mean striking back at the law of nature that had kept her from being a gymnast?"

"I doubt Michelle realized that that was it, but it was. The thing is, though, Vejay"—Vida wagged a finger at me—"if Michelle had gotten Ross, she would have been very disappointed. She didn't want *him;* she wanted her illusion of him."

"But would she have gone off with him?"

"Any time."

"Yesterday?"

"I wouldn't say no."

"And do you think Craig was aware of that?"

In the kitchen a chair scraped. The voices became louder but the words were still indistinct.

"I think," Vida said slowly and softly, "that Craig was well aware he was her second choice. In the beginning he thought he'd scored a coup in marrying Michelle. But success pales with reality."

"And now?"

"Things were rough the last year or two."

"So Michelle probably was ready for something else?"

"Maybe."

I could see Wescott's back through the doorway. He was standing tentatively, as if ready to move.

"Would she have tried something illegal? An illegal job she got from Ross? Or maybe held for Ross?"

"I—"

Wescott stepped back and Craig walked in.

I expected Wescott to warn me again, or at least ask what I was doing back here, but he didn't. Nodding to us, he walked to the door.

I hesitated, tempted to wait and ask Craig what he had said, then decided I needed to talk to Sheriff Wescott himself. "I'm just leaving too," I said, joining Wescott at the door. "I'll be in touch, Vida."

As soon as we were outside and the door had been shut behind us, I asked, "Does this visit mean you've changed your assessment of Michelle's death?"

"No, it doesn't."

"Then why were you here?"

"Fortunately, the Sheriff's Department isn't required to report every move to you."

"But you do see that it could be murder and by waiting you may be letting the suspect get away?"

We had reached the bottom of the stairs. He stopped and turned toward me. "It's after eight o'clock. I should have been off duty an hour ago. I'm tired. I'm thirsty. If you really want to talk, give me time to change out of uniform and meet me at the bar in half an hour."

The invitation was definitely not what I had been expecting from Sheriff Wescott, but it didn't shock me either. It wasn't in the same category that an invitation from Mr. Bobbs would have been. I knew Wescott found me a nuisance. His threats to arrest me were well within his power, but I didn't expect him to do that. There was something about me that he liked. And that gave me a bit of leeway in how far I could push him. What I didn't know was how much leeway. I'd know only when I'd exhausted it. Still, for the moment I was safe.

I realized as I stood in front of the mirror in my bathroom that I was applying eye shadow with more than usual care. I put on cleaner jeans and a warmer shirt, grabbed a sweater, and headed down the stairs.

Leaving my truck in the garage, I walked the few blocks to the bar.

The bar was officially titled Jim's, but, since it was the only establishment of its kind in town, we all referred to it as "the bar." It was a standard post-Depression watering hole, the type that could be found in any city across the country. To the left as I entered was a long mahogany bar with red stools and regular patrons on them. The floor space was filled with Formica-topped tables and plain wooden chairs. On the walls were pictures with waterfalls

that lit up and seascapes that moved. The only concession Jim had made to the California locale was to
add swinging doors. Jim himself was behind the bar.

Wescott beckoned from a table in the rear. Even
in the dim light his appearance startled me. Before
this I had seen him only in uniform. Now I realized
how much the tan color of that uniform accentuated
the unsmoothed lines of his nose and the wiry curl
of his light brown hair and mustache. Normally his
face looked like a sculpture awaiting its final sand-
ing. But now, in a teal blue shirt, it was the blue of
his eyes that stood out, and the rest of his face
seemed softened around them.

"Beer?" he asked, motioning me to the seat across
from him.

"Anchor Steam."

"Is that one of your San Francisco habits?" He
smiled, a disarming look. I recalled that smile from
the time I had told him about my years in San Francisco, my marriage to another account executive in
the public relations firm where I had worked, our
two years together, and our divorce when we realized how little there was between us. Those years,
the work, and the marriage had seemed all facade,
and when I left and moved to Henderson, I had tried
to change as much as I could, to turn my life inside
out and deal with the internal, the real. I had told
Wescott all about it in detail that later appalled me.

"My taste for Anchor Steam Beer's gotten more
firmly entrenched since I've been here," I said.
"Meter reading is thirsty work. Like sheriffing, I
imagine."

"Yes, but it doesn't look good for the sheriff to be
guzzling beer all day. And it's not that easy, anyway.

If you'll notice, no one is sitting at the tables around us. A sheriff is not a welcome sight in a bar."

"Even out of uniform?"

"You're never really out of uniform. If a fight broke out now I couldn't just watch. So that really settles the question of sheriffs in bars; it's as uncomfortable for us as it is for the other customers."

"So how come you suggested coming here tonight?"

"I wanted a beer and I wanted to talk—to you."

"Oh." Wescott had a way of focusing in on the object of his attention that was at once flattering and unnerving.

"How did you get involved in the Davidson death?" He waited expectantly.

Despite our surroundings and his show of interest, I believed, as he had said, that he was never totally out of uniform. I wasn't sure how much I wanted to tell the *sheriff*. "Michelle's aunt, Vida, is a meter reader. She asked me to look into it."

"Do you do whatever your colleagues ask you?" There was a touch of banter to his question.

"Vida's our union rep. She's the one who got me my pay back after they docked me for abusing sick leave, after *you* told Mr. Bobbs I had two drinks in a bar the day I called in sick!"

"That was an incidental in questioning him. You know I didn't mean to cost you money."

"I know. But Vida's the one who prepared for the hearings to get it back. She put a lot of time into that. I owe her. And besides, I may need her again."

He looked as if he expected more explanation.

"This morning," I went on, "I was arguing with Mr. Bobbs about a suggestion I made. He didn't want to deal with it, so he put it in a Follow-up folder. Do you know what that is?"

"No."

"It's legitimate procrastination. He dates a folder for whatever date he chooses, sticks whatever he wants to put off dealing with inside it, and gives it to the clerk. She doesn't bring it back to his desk until that date."

Wescott roared with laughter. A foursome seated two tables away stared. "That's great!" Wescott said. "I'd kill for a mechanism like that. I'd put all my drunk driving reports in a folder for next year."

"And the wonderful thing is that when they came back you could stick them right in another folder."

He finished his beer. "So why are you going to need your union?"

"Either because I am not Mr. Bobbs's favorite person and he may get tired of me bugging him, or because if he doesn't act on my suggestion soon, I'm going to file a grievance. It's a good suggestion. It's to the benefit of the employees and the company, too."

"What is it?"

I told him about the need for two-way radios.

"You're right. If you knew as much about the area as I do you'd be even more convinced." He looked directly at me, as if to reinforce his statement with his gaze.

The bar was filling up. Conversations began to blur into one indistinguishable rumble as the noise level rose. It was still early for the bar trade, but in another hour this place would be jammed. Conversation at any level would be a challenge.

Wescott took a long swallow of his beer. One mustache hair stood straight out beyond the wiry line of its compatriots. It caught on the rim of the glass. Wescott felt for it and pulled it out. Staring down at it, held between thumb and forefinger, he said, "I'd like to think you took my warning about steering clear of the Davidson woman's death to heart, but you didn't, did you?"

I started to speak, but he stopped me with a touch of the hand. "Vejay, suppose you are right and Michelle Davidson was murdered. Then, there's a murderer here. First you find the body, then you announce you're investigating, and then you plunk yourself right down in a hole where the murderer could do damn well as he pleased."

"It was the middle of the afternoon."

"And tonight when you go home, alone, it will be the middle of the night."

"Thanks a lot."

"I'm not trying to frighten you unnecessarily."

I fingered my glass. "It sounds like you're taking the possibility of murder more seriously than you were earlier."

"What I told you is still true. I don't know yet what caused her death. I think it was an accident. Everything points to that."

"What about the position of the body?"

"Your theory that she wouldn't fall backwards?"

"Yes. Michelle Davidson was a gymnast. She won a medal on the balance beam when she was in school."

"That was eight or ten years ago."

"But you don't forget how to balance. It becomes nearly instinctive. And Michelle still practiced. Ward McElvey told me she walked on her deck railing— backwards! There's a twenty-foot drop there."

"That's fine, but she was sober then. Guys around

here can drive any vehicle from a motorcycle to a moving van when they're sober. After a night of beer they crash their cars into the nearest tree."

"It's not the same. Michelle knew how to fall. She would never have landed flat on her back."

Wescott took a long breath. "If you believe that, you'd be wise to be careful."

"What about the bruise on her head?" I said, unwilling to have this very unsatisfactory discussion end with his warning. "Couldn't that have come from her murderer hitting her before throwing her in the sewer hole?"

"It also could have come from hitting her head against the edge of the pipe when she fell. She was close enough."

"Have they done an autopsy?"

"Not yet. It's Friday night."

"When, then?"

"Tomorrow," he snapped. "Look, I don't run the county. I don't have the coroner jumping to whenever I want him."

"Sorry," I said. "I should understand that."

He smiled. "Sure."

"Have your next beer on me."

"Is that a bribe?"

I signaled the waiter for another round and said to Wescott, "Just softening you up. Tell me about the Bohemian Connection."

"I thought that was common knowledge. I'm surprised that you don't know all about it."

Unable to resist the challenge, I said, "There are the drugs, liquor, rendezvous, and so forth."

"That's it. Most of it's small time, but well paid. Some people rent their places during Bohemian Week. It's all under the table. A little tax-free income. Of course, they don't tell us. We've burst in on one or two tête-à-têtes because we knew the houses were supposed to be empty—the owners informed us they were going to be gone for months but didn't tell us about their Bohemian Week arrangement. And then there are the actual housebreakings."

Thinking of Maria Keneally's house, I asked, "For housebreaking, wouldn't a place need to be secluded?"

"Right. The Connection knows the owner is away and just breaks in. Most of those places are back in the hills where the nearest neighbor is half a mile away. It's rare to have a really secluded house near town. And the one thing the Connections have always been careful about is cleaning up afterwards. We don't know how many houses they've used because we get only one or two complaints. In the other cases the Connection has put everything back to normal."

"Except the broken window?"

"Well . . ." He shrugged. "Lots of people are careless. You wouldn't need to break a window to get in." He looked directly at me, tacitly suggesting that I knew more than the average woman about such things. "And a lot of windows get broken innocently. If a homeowner discovers a window broken but everything inside the house as he left it, he doesn't call the sheriff, he calls a glazier."

"Do you think the Bohemian Connection makes enough money to be worth killing for?"

The waiter arrived with our beers. Wescott swished a mouthful around and nodded solemnly in mock approval. He put the glass down and said, "Killing is like anything else, very individual. I doubt you or I would find the money worth a life, but then how much would you need to protect before you'd kill for it? For some folks that's not much. But it's rarely just money. There are other, stronger concerns. If Ross Remson were still the Connection and we were talking about him, I would say that the notoriety was more important than the cash."

"Important enough to kill for?"

"I don't know. But I also don't think you should take the chance of finding out." He paused. "Am I making myself clear?"

Ignoring that, I said, "Ross Remson was the Bohemian Connection until he left, right?"

"What?"

The noise level had risen. I leaned closer and repeated my question.

"That was before my time. There was never any proof, but the department knew Remson was the Connection."

"Who took over when he left?"

"We don't know. Remson was flamboyant. He wanted the attention of people suspecting him. Whoever came after has been much more low-key."

"And it's not a priority for you. Particularly if the Connection keeps a low profile."

He didn't answer, but I could tell from his irritated expression that I had touched on a sore spot.

"It could be a woman, couldn't it?"

Now he smiled. "Are you considering moonlighting? You've got the perfect job for finding out what homes are empty and how long they're going to be that way."

"It could be a woman though, couldn't it?"

His smile disappeared. "What are you after?

Look, I asked you here as a friend. As a friend I warned you. I don't want to see you end up in the space Michelle Davidson vacated this afternoon. I also don't want to be pumped."

I sighed. "I appreciate your concern, really. I know you're aware of the dangers of this area. But I haven't been racing around on the hottest day of the year, badgering people, because I had nothing better to do on my afternoon off. Michelle's family deserves to have her murderer found. They need the question of how she died cleared up. If you would investigate Michelle's death, I'd take your advice and spend the weekend on the beach."

Wescott stared at me with the same iciness I recalled from the interrogation in his office in Guerneville. I looked away.

"Oh my god!"

"What?"

"That man, the one who just walked out of the bathroom, that's Ross Remson."

Wescott didn't move.

"Aren't you going to do something?"

"There's no reason—"

I jumped up.

Wescott grabbed my arm.

"That's Ross. Father Calloway saw him with Michelle last night. He was behind her neighbor's house this afternoon. I've spent hours looking for him. Let me go."

Still holding my arm, he said, "If you're right, then this man is dangerous."

Ross stood at the bar, his back to us.

"Are you going to let him get away because he might be dangerous?"

"Look—"

I jerked loose and started for the bar. "Ross," I called.

Ross didn't move.

I reached out to touch his shoulder.

Wescott pushed in front of me. He flashed his shield and grabbed Ross's arm. "Sheriff's Department. Come outside quietly, Remson."

"Hey, wait!"

"I said outside."

The bar was silent. No one moved.

"Officer, you're making a mistake."

"Outside!"

"Just let me talk, Officer."

Wescott shoved him through the swinging doors. I followed.

"Hands up against the building. Spread your feet." Wescott moved in behind him and patted him down. "No weapon," he muttered.

"Listen, Officer. Listen to me. You're making a mistake. Look at my driver's license. My name is David Sugarbaker."

I had heard about pockets in time, and the concept that time could be stretched like a rubber band, but rarely had a minute extended so long as the one after David George Sugarbaker handed his driver's license to Sheriff Wescott. We stood in the alley next to the bar where Wescott had parked. At the edge of the sidewalk by North Bank Road a small crowd of onlookers formed, watching as Wescott called in for a make on the license.

The call came back after that minute. Sugarbaker was clean. And he was Sugarbaker, not Ross Remson.

Now that I could examine his face, the differences were obvious. Superficially he looked a lot like Ross —both were six feet tall, both had sandy hair that was just curly enough to notice—but Ross had a space between his front teeth and a sardonic look about him. Sugarbaker had neither. His teeth were even, his stance shaky. And his expression teetered between anger and fear. He looked like a dog who had soiled the parlor rug.

And Wescott looked like the dog's owner. "How long have you lived at this address, Sugarbaker?" he demanded.

"Well, I guess you could say eight months." His words weren't slurred yet, but he wasn't sober either.

"What do you mean, 'you guess'? Don't you know how long you've lived there? Maybe you don't really live there?"

"I do. It's just that I've lived there before. I didn't know if you wanted that time too."

"So you stayed there before, you moved away, and now you're back, is that it?"

Sugarbaker glanced nervously at the crowd. "Yes," he mumbled.

"What kind of place is this, Sugarbaker? What kind of people live there? Any the Sheriff's Department knows?"

Sugarbaker didn't say anything. I came close to praying his house was crammed with wanted felons. Only a discovery of that magnitude could rescue this fiasco.

"Who lives there?" Wescott repeated.

Sugarbaker's voice was even lower than before. "My parents."

"What?"

"I live with my parents. It's just been since my divorce. It doesn't cost much. I have my own entrance. It's almost like an apartment."

From the crowd behind me I could hear a few chuckles followed by the rumble of conversation.

Wescott spun toward them. "This isn't a side show! Move along." Turning back to Sugarbaker, he said, "Where are you staying locally?"

The crowd had broken up. Sugarbaker's voice seemed louder as he said, "I don't know. I was going to check in somewhere later. I thought about the Winding Road Inn."

Wescott swallowed. "Well, Mr. Sugarbaker," he said almost paternally, "let me give you a bit of advice. You're not in any condition to drive that far.

I'm sure you don't want to be a danger on the road. You'd do much better to choose one of the quieter spots within walking distance, like Genelle's."

"Yessir."

"Good." As he turned back toward the car, Wescott had that condescending look of a lawman who has given the gift of a warning instead of a ticket. It was only when he turned to me that his fury was evident. And that was just for a split second. Then he climbed into his car and left.

Both Sugarbaker and I stood watching the car pull away. At least, I thought, he didn't ask Wescott who he had mistaken him for. He was so nervous he seemed to have forgotten about that. He acted as if Wescott had a good reason to arrest him, as if he had something to hide—perhaps living with his parents.

He turned and stared down at me. "Fucking asshole!" he exclaimed. "What kind of place is this? Who does he fucking think he is? Dragging people out of public establishments with no reason."

The transformation from the fearful, servile man of a minute ago was almost total. Now Sugarbaker did look like Ross Remson. His eyes had that same crazed intensity, his jaw the same hard set.

"Who did he think I was anyway? Some punk? Somebody who's going to upset the big shots here this weekend? Huh? Huh?"

I tried to decide how best to explain what had happened. Should I admit that it was my fault? That I was the one who mistook him for Ross? Would he be calmer for knowing that? Or would it make him even angrier to discover that it wasn't even the sheriff who had made the mistake?

"False arrest! That's it, false arrest!"

"You weren't arrested."

"Well, false imprisonment then."

"False being yanked out of a bar?" I offered.

"What? Huh?" He looked down at me and the pugnacious set of his jaw eased. "God knows what that jerk would have done if you hadn't been here."

It took me a moment to realize that he hadn't connected me with Wescott. There was no reason he should have. Before Wescott grabbed his arm we had been behind him, our conversation covered by the noise of the bar. After that he had other things to think about.

"Are you a reporter or something?" he asked me. "Or do you just keep a citizen's watch on the sheriff?"

"Neither really."

He paused, then smiled, a knowing look. "Just watching out for me then?"

"You remind me of someone," I said.

He looked at once surprised, a bit deflated, yet curious. "You know you're the second woman who's said that."

Surely he meant Michelle. She must have mentioned it to him last night. Despite the heat of the day it was chilly now. I pulled my sweater tighter around me.

"Cold, huh? Look, the least I can do is buy you a drink. I can sure use one after dealing with that jerk. Boy, can you believe that? Does that happen a lot here, that kind of harassment?"

His little encounter with the sheriff was definitely a subject I didn't want to reopen. On the very slim possibility that he might run into the sheriff again, I didn't want him to be able to quote one word of mine on that topic. I walked back into the bar and asked for a beer.

On a less busy night my reentry with the man Wescott and I had hustled out of there minutes earlier might have attracted some comment, but if anyone remembered it tonight amidst the shouts and laughter and clanking of glasses, they didn't mention it loud enough for me to hear. I followed Sugarbaker to a table near the back of the bar. I would have preferred one against the wall where it would have been quieter, but those had been snatched up by the few other people who had intentions of being heard. Sugarbaker pulled out a chair for me and sat in the opposite one, facing into the room.

Before he could return to the topic of the sheriff, I checked my assumption, asking, "The woman who said you looked like someone else, who was she?"

It took him a moment to readjust his thoughts. "A complainant."

A complainant! How bad could my luck be? "Are you a lawyer?" No wonder he had thought of false arrest.

"No."

"A legal assistant?"

"No."

"Well?"

"I'm a field investigator for the Department of Environmental Health."

The mosquito man! I laughed so hard the beer slopped over the edge of my glass and onto my hand.

Sugarbaker, the mosquito man, stared. "What's so funny?"

"Sorry," I said. And when I was more composed,

I said, "You investigate things like complaints about mosquitoes, right?"

"Uh-huh."

"One of my friends had a complaint about mosquitoes—Michelle Davidson on Half Hill Road."

"Hey, that's her. She's been calling in every month since Christmas."

"Every month?"

"Residents are only allowed to complain once a month."

I laughed again. Was this rule Environmental Health's answer to Follow-up? Did each bureaucracy have its own special system for avoiding having to deal with grievances? I suspected Mr. Bobbs would gladly trade Follow-up for the joy of restricting me to one complaint a month.

"I'll bet that limits your work."

He smiled tentatively. "It's a practical rule. Our investigations take time. You have to come out and look the situation over. That's what I was doing yesterday, looking at your friend's garage. Then I had to take a sample—"

"So you met Michelle then?"

Now he did smile. It wasn't hard to see what he thought of Michelle. "Real looker, your friend. Real interested in her problem."

"The mosquito larvae?"

"Yes."

"So what did you conclude?"

He took a swallow of his beer and leaned forward. Behind him three men pushed between the tables. To the right a group burst into laughter. It was all I could do to hear Sugarbaker. I leaned closer.

"Real nice lady," he said.

"Did you make a date to see her last night?"

"Nah. It wasn't a date. Nothing like that. We just happened to meet. She has a husband, you know, not that that would have stopped her. She seemed, well, you know, hot to trot." He finished his beer. His eyes were beginning to droop now but his speech gave no hint he had been drinking. He ordered another round even though my glass was still half full.

"I don't want to sound like I think I'm irresistible. I got over that a few years ago." He laughed. "Divorce makes you realize that you're not everyone's taste."

"Indeed."

"You divorced too?"

"Yes. It's the California way."

"How long?"

"Few years."

"Oh. Mine was final two months ago. That's how come I'm staying with my folks. Donna, my ex, took everything—the house, the car, the cats. We didn't live in California. It wasn't a community property state. If I'd known we were going to get divorced, I would have moved back here. Then I'd have a place to live or something to drive."

Next to the sheriff, this was the last topic I wanted to hear about. My own divorce had been relatively easy. Unlike the apparent bonfire the Sugarbakers had had, mine had been more like sweeping away the ash. I asked, "Do you think it was accidental, Michelle's seeing you last night?"

He shrugged. "I wasn't all that surprised. Her husband works late Thursday nights. She told me."

Two more beers arrived. Sugarbaker poured a glass and downed half of it. "Odd though."

"How?"

"Couldn't figure her out. I mean she sat there staring at me like she couldn't wait, you know. Then she'd shake herself out of it and look at me like she'd never seen me before. And she'd ask me about her complaint."

"What did you tell her?"

"About her complaint, you mean?" He gave his head a quick shake and seemed to pull himself back a notch closer to sobriety. "She had a reasonable gripe. I told her that. She wanted to know how she could speed things up. I'm not supposed to tell complainants to do that, you know. But she had this real clear complaint, so I told her, 'Get some clout.' That's what I said. 'Call your congressman.' Boy you get one of them bugging the department for you and wham!—your complaint is number one."

I took a sip of my beer.

"That's what I should do about that jerk, the sheriff. I can call my congressman. And I can sue, too. What do you think?"

"Did Michelle say she would contact her congressman?"

He tried to open his eyes wide but the lids moved only halfway, then closed back to where they had been, so that his eyes were nearly slits. It was as if his eyes absorbed all the effects of the alcohol and his speech none. "Odd thing," he said. "She said her congressman would be here, in this town, this Sunday to give a speech. Then she laughed."

"Laughed!"

"Yeah. She said he'd get a good audience. She said the last congressman who spoke here blocked traffic or something and the people burned down his podium." Sugarbaker was sounding less sober by the moment.

"Did Michelle say she'd ask the congressman about her problem?"

He giggled. "She said after the heat he might get from the rest of the people here, he'd be glad to talk to her about her mosquito larvae." He downed the rest of his beer.

"What happened then—after she told you about the congressman?"

He eyed me suspiciously. "We talked. Nothing else. We were getting on real good. I told her I could tell her what to say to her congressman. We could get together, plan what she should say."

"When were you going to do that?"

"We could have then, that night. I had this motel room—"

"Did you ask her?"

He picked up the glass and stared into it. He looked like he was having a hard time using those almost-closed eyes.

I repeated my question louder.

"Well, no. Odd thing. All of a sudden she gets real mad. I mean you don't stare at the person you're talking to all the time, do you? I mean, you look at other people, and some of them are women, right?"

"Yes?"

"I'll admit it, I was looking at this blonde, at the bar. She had these dark blue eyes and this wild blond hair. She was wearing overalls, with this wild blond hair." He paused so long I thought he was about to pass out, but he pulled himself together and said, "Then, all of a sudden Michelle gets mad. She says, 'Do you find her attractive?' Just like a schoolteacher or something. I say, 'Not bad.' And she gets up and stomps out, just like that. Not a word."

I restrained my urge to comment, "Odd thing." Instead, I asked, "What did you do after Michelle left?"

"I sat there, then I was going to hit on the blonde, but she left, and then there was this brunette, but . . . I went back to my motel. But I'm not staying there tonight. No, sir. I told them what they could do with their cesspool of a place." He put both hands on the table, started to push himself up, then dropped back into his chair. "They sell bottles of wine here. We could get a bottle. Do you live around here?"

"I do, but I can't ask you to come with me."

"But we get along so well. We could have a little fun. No commitment, no ties, just fun."

"I'm not the one you're looking for. But you're in the right spot for looking this weekend." I stood up.

His face reddened. "Hey, you don't need to take that Miss Priss—"

"Thanks for the beer."

Once outside I hesitated. I didn't want a drunken Sugarbaker staggering after me to my house, which he could have easily done since I was on foot. That was part of the reason I chose to head for the café. The other equally pressing matter was that it had been a long time since lunch, substantial though it had been. And the prospect of the café's wonderful fried eggs, chorizo sausage, and sauerkraut was too good to pass up.

The café was probably the one place in town that was fairly empty. At nine-thirty on this Friday night most celebrants were in the bar, or the lounge of one of the fancier motels. Few people in the Russian River Resort Area on the first night of Bohemian Week were thinking about sauerkraut. I ordered and took my favorite table in the back.

I had come here for breakfast before work many mornings when I had more time than ambition. Recently I had discovered I'd become enough of a regular to call ahead and have my eggs and kraut waiting as I rushed in, which solved my problem on those days when I had neither time nor ambition. By now it never occurred to the cooks that I ate anything else.

Two couples and a family occupied other tables. One of the children surveyed the jukebox selections, then stalked back to his table. Obviously he was not

an aficionado of early country music. No Mother
Maybelle on the zither for him.

The fluorescent lights reflected off the white tables
and the tweed linoleum floor. It seemed as bright as
morning now.

With disgust I thought of David Sugarbaker. It
wasn't that he'd been drunk; not even that he'd been
drunkenly surly. His sin was not being Ross Remson.

It was hard for me to accept the fact that Ross
Remson was not in Henderson. Wherever he had
gone the last time he had left town, either he was
still there hiding from his San Francisco cronies, or
he'd moved on to some place safer. Wherever he
was, he wasn't here.

Briefly, I considered the possibility that he could
be here—that both Ross Remson and David
Sugarbaker could be in the same town. But that possibility was too remote to waste time on. No, the
man I had seen by Michelle's house was David
Sugarbaker, and the reason he was there was to look
at her mosquito larvae.

So Ross Remson had not killed Michelle. Michelle
may or may not have become the Bohemian Connection, but Ross had not killed her to get the job
back.

Maybe Michelle was not the Bohemian Connection. Maybe the Bohemian Connection had nothing
to do with her death. Maybe she hadn't even been
murdered.

I slumped back in my chair. Could it be that Sheriff Wescott was right—Michelle's death had been an
accident? The reason I had been suspicious from the
beginning was because I saw Ross's picture, then
saw "Ross" behind Ward and Jenny's house, and

later saw him staring down at the sewer hole before he disappeared. But now that there was another explanation—David Sugarbaker had been checking out mosquito larvae—was there any reason to believe Michelle had been killed? Had I annoyed people, wasted my day, and made an enemy of the local sheriff for no reason at all?

My eggs, sauerkraut, and chorizo arrived with a slab of heated black bread. A non-meter reader might have been too depressed to eat, but I dug in.

What *did* I know had happened? Michelle had met David Sugarbaker when he came out in the afternoon to look at her garage. She had asked Father Calloway to let her off when she spotted him in town. Why? She knew he wasn't Ross. Was she in the habit of drinking with male acquaintances? Vida, of course, denied that. The impression I had was that Michelle would have gone with Ross any time, but not with just any man. But that wasn't the message Sugarbaker got. I wondered what shape he was in last night. How reliable was his judgment? Were his eyes open enough to see Michelle's reactions? Or did he see what he wanted to see? Still, as Vida had said, Michelle wouldn't have gone off with some strange man the night before the anti-hookers' demonstration.

David Sugarbaker had said she asked him about speeding up the response to her complaint. Might she have simply stopped for another look at this man who resembled Ross? Then whatever conversation there was would have just been filler. Could it be that Michelle had led him on—as he had said, looking at him as adoringly as she would have gazed at Ross—only to shake herself back to reality. Had she agreed to have him take her home and then rebuffed him at the foot of the stairs by the sewer hole? Drunk and angry, had he pushed her in?

It was possible. But if he had killed her, why was he hanging around here? Why wasn't he putting as much distance between the sewer hole and himself as possible? Did he think it would look better for him to stay here as if nothing had happened? Did he have other cesspools and larvae to investigate?

I would have to talk to David Sugarbaker again. I dunked a forkful of sauerkraut in egg yolk.

Who else benefited from Michelle's death? Craig? He and Michelle weren't getting along. She resented Alison working at the shop. Nothing out of the ordinary for a young couple. That was grounds for a separate vacation, but hardly for murder.

Ward and Jenny McElvey? Both of them found Michelle a nuisance. There was a chance she could have forced them to hook up to the sewer sooner than Ward wanted. But you don't kill your neighbor so you can use your cesspool two months longer. And for Jenny, who seemed as estranged from the whole cesspool dispute as she was from her brother Ross (indeed uninterested in anything more mundane than her art), Michelle was merely a pest that could be swatted away.

And Alison? Was she afraid of losing her job? Perhaps. But Alison had traveled; she had worked other places. She had created this job from nothing. There was no reason she couldn't do the same elsewhere.

I piled a forkful of sauerkraut atop a piece of chorizo and managed to balance an inch of egg on that before I brought it warily to my mouth.

Alison? Was it Alison that Sugarbaker had seen in the bar? A woman with dark blue eyes, wild blond hair, and overalls—that described Alison. Michelle's reaction made sense if it had been Alison. No other woman would have made her so angry. If Sugarbaker had been looking at Jenny or Vida or me, would Michelle have been annoyed? Surely she wouldn't have cared enough to stomp out. But seeing him ignore her to gaze upon Alison, just as Ross had left Henderson and lived with Alison, would have been enough to trigger her anger.

I bit into the warm black bread.

Alison? Alison had gone to a lot of trouble to get a job in Henderson. Why? Because she liked the area? That was reason enough. The whole Russian River Resort Area had an appealing woodsyness, a vacation atmosphere, while still being close enough to San Francisco for a trip to the theater. But did Alison have stronger reasons? Why had Ross brought her up here? Was it to give her the Bohemian Connection job? Had he brought her here to introduce her to the people she would need to meet, to show her around so she would know how to get to the cocaine dealers and the empty houses?

But that was eight years ago. Why had Alison waited all this time to move here? And how had the Connection work been handled in the meantime? Could Ross have done it from out of town? Could he have known what houses were vacant and where the owners were and been sure that no owner would pop up unexpectedly? Could he have handled emergency demands? The only way Ross could have done that from outside was to have scaled down the operation to Bohemian Week only . . . or have an assistant in Henderson. And the likely assistant was Michelle.

So, had Michelle run the Bohemian Connection in

Ross's absence? Then, this year, had Ross blithely sold or given the business to Alison? If Alison had arrived to take over, Michelle would have been outraged.

If the Connection were anyone but Alison, Michelle might have accepted a financial arrangement. She might even have agreed to be pushed out. But Alison was different. Michelle resented her. She wouldn't let Alison steal the Connection. And Alison would never be safe as long as Michelle knew she was the Connection. She was the one person Michelle would gladly turn in to the sheriff.

If Alison wanted to secure the Bohemian Connection job, she would have had to kill Michelle.

I recalled Alison at Maria Keneally's house by the cemetery. That would be a perfect spot for the Connection to use. It was secluded and the owner was overseas for the summer. Alison may have been there earlier this afternoon to get it set up.

I finished the sauerkraut and chorizo and mopped up the last drops of yolk with the black bread. It was clear to me that before I came to a decision, I would have to be sure that Sugarbaker was telling me the truth about Michelle's departure—that he hadn't left with her—and I would have to see if Alison was the woman he saw at the bar. I paid for my dinner and headed outside. The sidewalk was nearly empty now. There was no place to walk to. Even on this weekend the shops along North Bank Road closed early. No one in town for a *fun* weekend would be patronizing the hardware store or the grocery at ten-thirty. Fischer's Ice Cream was still open. There was still a line. Otherwise, the only populated establishment was the bar. It was amazing how quiet the town proper was.

This was about the same time that Michelle had left the bar last night, if Sugarbaker was to be believed. The town would have been even more deserted, it being Thursday. And once she left North Bank Road, there would have been no street lights, no one on foot. She would have been alone, oblivious to the danger.

The noise from the bar greeted me twenty feet away. Through the swinging doors, I could see the crowd. I had to pull one of the doors toward me to avoid pushing it into a pair of customers.

Inside, people filled all the chairs, all the bar stools, stood between tables, and leaned against the walls. They stood two and three deep at the bar. Sugarbaker was nowhere in sight. Had he found the right lady and gone?

I spotted Jim at the far end of the bar and began to edge my way between drinkers toward him. The smoke was dense. The clatter of glasses and the roar of conversation made anything below a scream inaudible.

I pushed my way to the corner of the bar. "Jim," I hollered.

Jim didn't move.

I repeated my call. It wasn't until the fourth one that he came toward me.

He grinned. "Vejay. I don't see you in here for days, and then suddenly you can't stay away. You want a beer?"

"No, I've had enough."

"Now there's something I don't often hear." His grin got wider. "Well, if you're not here for a beer are you looking for another man to round out your evening?"

I thought no one had noticed. I'd forgotten Jim's

reputation for knowing every flirtation, every innu-
endo that passed lips in his bar. Jim's was one of the
few bars in the area that was rarely mentioned in the
Sheriff's Report in the newspaper. Jim caught argu-
ments early, before bottles became weapons.

"I'm counting on your eagle eye."

"Okay," he shouted, "but I don't have much
time." He indicated the crowd pushing toward the
bar for drinks.

"Right. You saw the man I was with tonight—not
the sheriff—the other one."

"Yes?"

"Did you see him in here last night?"

"Yes."

"With Michelle Davidson?"

"Yes."

"Did he leave with her?"

"You jealous?"

Apparently Jim hadn't heard of Michelle's death
yet.

"No. Believe me. I'll explain when you're not so
rushed. But it's important. And I am a regular customer."

"Okay, okay. No, your boyfriend stayed after she
left. Pretty teed off he was, too. But he got over that
fast. Tried to put the make on a couple other
women. He was pretty far gone. I thought I was
going to have to take action, but then he staggered
out of his own accord." Jim turned back to his customers.

"One more thing, Jim."

He turned only his head toward me.

"Alison Barluska, do you know her?"

He nodded.

"Was she in here last night?"

He hesitated. I could tell from his expression that if we had been alone, he would have had some questions for me before providing an answer. But now, rushed as he was, he just said, "Yes."

"When?"

But he had already turned and headed for the beer glasses.

I pushed my way back through the crowd.

At a table along the side wall, three meter readers waved and called. I waved back but kept moving for the door.

Once outside I turned toward my house, walking quickly through town to the stop light and then along the steep-sided road that suddenly seemed very dark.

If Alison was in the bar last night, then she wasn't with Craig. Why had he insisted that she was with him constantly until he went home? What was he hiding? As I walked through the darkness, I realized that I would have to deal with Craig tomorrow. I would have to challenge that tightly controlled temper of his and find out why he had lied.

Contrary to Sheriff Wescott's expectation, I had quite a decent sleep. I was exhausted. I was used to physically grueling days, ones where I climbed up and down hillsides, trudged up steep driveways, and made my way through overgrown yards hoping I hadn't missed any spot of skin when I had applied the ImunOak. Meter reading has its drawbacks, but for minimizing stress there is nothing like walking for eight hours and doing a job at which you are competent. Even personal crises seem manageable at the end of a strenuous route. But sitting in my truck in the heat all day and emerging only to provoke people was another thing. By the time I got home it took all my strength to climb into the bathtub.

And when I woke in the morning it was later than I had planned—after eight. Still half asleep, I decided I would make breakfast first, then deal with the very unpleasant task of confronting Craig.

Craig had lied to me when he insisted he and Alison were together until he went home Thursday night. He was hiding something. He was protecting himself, or Alison, or both. No wonder he had been so hesitant about asking me to look into Michelle's death. That he agreed to it at all was a testimonial to Vida's influence.

I showered, toweled off, and left my hair wet. I

dawdled over my makeup, procrastinating. And breakfast—I couldn't face it at all.

The parking lot at Davidson's Plants was empty except for Craig's car and the shop truck. On the sliding glass door was a Closed sign. Peering in, I spotted Craig adjusting a container of plants. I banged on the glass.

"Craig," I called. "It's Vejay."

He turned, and from his immediate, unguarded expression, I thought he would walk away. But almost instantly his face changed to that of the pleasant, helpful man his customers dealt with. He pulled open the door.

"I'm not doing business today," he said. "But there are some things that can't be put off. And sitting home wasn't going to make me feel better. The kids are still with Michelle's sister. They don't know. I saw them last night. They're better off there."

"When are you going to tell them?"

He sank back against the counter. "I don't know. Soon, I guess. I don't want to have them hear it somewhere else. But I just couldn't last night."

"It's lucky you have so many relatives around here."

Craig nodded. He looked tired and rumpled, as if he'd slept in his clothes. Even his beard looked slept in. I recalled thinking that he was wiry and strong, but now his muscles seemed to weigh down his body. His brown hair was greasy from not having been washed, and the beginning of a bald spot showed through on top.

"It's going to be awful for the kids. Michelle spent so much time with them. I couldn't because of the shop. I couldn't make money and have time to be home too. I had to be here. I had to go to professional meetings; I had to go to the flower market—I mean, before Jenny started doing it. I just couldn't spend the time with the kids."

"That's pretty normal," I said.

"Maybe, but it won't make it any easier on them now." Turning toward the tall vases of cut flowers on the far end of the counter beside the African violets, Craig said, "Used to be we could just get mums and dahlias and an occasional iris. But now with all the gays here, they want variety, they want exotic." He moved a bunch of yellow trumpet-shaped flowers that seemed plenty exotic to me.

Seeing how upset Craig was, I hesitated momentarily. Then, taking a breath, I said, "Craig, where were you Thursday night?"

He turned back toward me, his brows lifted in question.

"You said you were here with Alison, all evening, until nearly midnight. You weren't, were you?"

His jaw tightened, but he didn't say anything.

"Alison was in the bar."

"She was only gone a few minutes."

"How long?"

"I don't know. What difference does it make? I was here."

"You said you were *together* all evening."

He was still holding the plastic vase of yellow flowers. His fingers pressed tighter against it.

"I asked you if either of you went out for a beer and you said you were too busy—the books didn't balance. You don't lie for no reason, Craig. You don't lie about the night your wife was killed."

"Michelle wasn't killed! She just died."

"Then why didn't you tell me the truth? You had

your car here Thursday night. That's why Michelle needed a ride. You could have left the truck in the parking lot and the light on in the office to suggest you were here. *You* could have driven anywhere."

"You better leave, Vejay." His voice was controlled now, but his knuckles were white.

"I'll go when you tell me what really happened Thursday night."

"You—" His lips pressed hard against each other.

"You and Michelle weren't getting along. She'd been drinking with the duplicate of her old boyfriend. She left the bar and was killed. And that's the exact time Alison was not with you. That's the time you lied about."

"I said you'd better leave." He stepped back. That reining in was more ominous than a move toward me.

"Maybe you were here. Maybe it was Alison you were protecting. Maybe she didn't come back here after she left the bar."

"Vejay."

"Or maybe both of you. Maybe this business—"

He hurled the plastic vase. It smashed into the wall behind me. He grabbed me by the shoulders, yanking me off my feet, and threw me through the open door so hard that I landed sprawled against a potted spruce five feet away. He pulled the glass door closed.

When I recovered enough to stand up, he was nowhere in sight.

I brushed the dirt off the seat of my jeans and walked through the parking lot. I wasn't hurt. Craig could have hurt me, but he hadn't. A smaller woman like Michelle might have been bruised. A less sturdy woman might have been frightened. Vida had told me about Craig's temper, but what she hadn't said, perhaps hadn't known, was that he could intimidate physically while still under some control. I wondered if he had learned that during his years with Michelle.

Twice I had seen Craig faced with my demands. In his house with Vida yesterday evening, when his only available weapons were words, he couldn't fight back. He acquiesced grudgingly, but he did as Vida told him. Today, again, he couldn't argue. Maybe, he didn't know how. Maybe he had never won with words. Physical force was his only recourse.

Still, I didn't know if he was capable of killing. And I didn't know where he'd been Thursday night.

I walked into the café. It was early yet for Saturday morning breakfast. Weekdays saw a number of regulars and semi-regulars rushing in before work, but Saturday most of the locals ate at home and most of the tourists weren't up. So this morning there was just me and two women sitting at a table by the wall.

Had it not been Bohemian Week, and had I not had Michelle's anti-hookers' group in the back of my mind, I might have assumed they were merely tourists from Southern California. Neither looked like the stereotypical prostitute. One was brunette, the other blond—not platinum, but a darker, streaked, almost natural-looking shade. Their makeup was carefully done, just a bit obvious. Both wore shorts, a clear sign that they were not Northern Californians—not on a foggy morning like this —and the blonde wore a sleeveless front-button T-shirt, with the buttons open just far enough to

show a strip of untanned cleavage. Both were freez-
ing.

I walked over to them. "The best place to get
sweaters is the hardware store."

The blonde looked up suspiciously. The brunette,
who was eating one of the café's superb blueberry
buttermilk biscuits, continued to chew.

"There are a couple of dress shops here and in
Guerneville, but they carry those light summer
sweaters that don't do anything in this weather except remind you how cold you are."

The brunette glanced at the prominent goose-
bumps on her arm. "I don't know why I can't remember. Every time I come up north I freeze." She
had a trace of a Midwestern accent.

Marty, the weekend waiter, and the café's token
gay, plunked my eggs and kraut on the table.

"You don't mind?" I asked perfunctorily as I sat
down.

The blonde shrugged. She was just drinking coffee. She looked from my plate to my midsection and
back.

"I get a lot of exercise," I said.

"Tell us about the sweaters," the brunette insisted. "Where do we get them and how soon?"

"The hardware store, Gresham's, is right down
the street. You have to go through all the pipes and
tools to the back where they have the overalls and
the flannel shirts and those thick ragg sweaters with
the shawl collars. And"—I looked down at my
watch—"they should open in about twenty minutes."

"Thanks," the brunette said. "I was beginning to
think of those mountain climbers who died on Everest."

The blonde sat silent, looking both bored and wary. There was more similarity between the brunette and I than the two of them. The blonde, I suspected, didn't know where Everest was. And if you asked her about scaling, she would have thought of a dermatologist.

I hated to endanger this moment of friendliness, a commodity getting rarer in my life, but I said, "Can I ask you one question?" Before they could answer, I continued. "You've probably heard of an anti-prostitution demonstration outside the Grove scheduled for this weekend. Do you think whether or not that was held would affect what goes on here?"

"How would I know?" It was the blonde.

I waited, looking toward her companion.

She seemed to be considering.

"If you had to guess . . ." I prompted.

She nodded slowly. "If I had inside knowledge on such matters, I would feel sure that very little would affect things. Certainly not a protest. If protests made a difference, the Grove would have been closed years ago. The men in there are too big to be bothered by these nuisances. Why do you ask?"

"The woman who was to lead the protest died."

The brunette shook her head. "Don't waste your time thinking that's the reason. A crime of any sort is the last thing anyone here for Bohemian Week wants."

"I'm sure you're right."

We sat a moment in uncomfortable silence. The muffin was gone. The coffee cups drained. Marty arrived with their check.

"You don't mind?" the brunette said, skillfully mocking my earlier words.

As they got up, I started on my eggs. They didn't

taste as good as they had last night. I didn't know
what Craig had been doing Thursday night. I didn't
know if his story about Alison just being gone a few
minutes was true or not. If it were night now I could
have asked Jim at the bar how long Alison had been
there. The only other person who would know was
David Sugarbaker. To find out I would have to deal
with him at his motel. At nine A.M. he wouldn't be as
chipper as I was.

CHAPTER

14

Even though the Pacific fog now masked the sun, and people wore jeans and heavy sweaters, Henderson was still a resort town on a Saturday morning. Most of the visiting families were from the San Francisco Bay area or farther north; to them, the fog that rolled in with the late afternoon breezes and cleared mid-morning was normal summer weather. They knew it would be sunny by noon. And here in Henderson, it would be hot.

North Bank Road was already bumper-to-bumper with families heading toward their motels or out to Jenner by the sea. The café had begun to fill as I paid for my breakfast. Shops were opening. There was even a line outside Fischer's Ice Cream. No sun over the yardarm for ice cream buffs.

Genelle's Family Cabins were about a block past town on North Bank Road, just before North Bank reverted to being River Road. I walked along the sidewalk toward them. Near the end of the block a car was double-parked, causing the rest of the line of traffic to edge into the oncoming lane. As I came nearer, I recognized Ward McElvey's Pacer. The sloping metal supports between its large windows gave it the appearance of an Easter basket. Ward was getting out—into traffic.

A horn honked. A woman leaned out the passenger window of an old sedan and yelled something that was masked by the street noises. Jenny got out the other side of the Pacer, seemingly oblivious to the altercation, and began unloading her easel, umbrella, charcoal, paper, and light. Ward pulled out the chairs and carried them around to the sidewalk.

They didn't notice me as I passed. I looked down from the raised sidewalk into the car. It was roomy, almost like a glass-covered pickup truck, with the same disadvantages. A trunk was the thing I missed most with my truck.

Walking along the road after the sidewalk ended took all my concentration. The same cars that Ward had delayed gunned their engines as soon as they passed him, not expecting to find a pedestrian on the two-lane road. I walked as close as possible to the hillside, and even so, twice I had to fling myself back against the sandbags that the sewer company had left to shore up the hillside. Ivy, oxalis, and wild blackberry plants covered them already, and probably poison oak.

Genelle's Family Cabins were fifteen-foot wooden squares with fresh paint and windowboxes. Sheriff Wescott had been kind to suggest this motel. There were plenty of seedier ones around. I walked up to the desk in the main cabin. There were cut flowers next to the register—yesterday's flowers, Genelle herself explained, since the plant shop was closed today. A death, you know. I nodded. And that was all the helpful information I got. There was no David Sugarbaker registered there. No single man at all had registered after ten last night. Thanking her, I headed back to town.

It hadn't occurred to me that I wouldn't find Sugarbaker, but now it was a real possibility. This was a resort area. Motels were one of the things we had in abundance. I could spend the entire day going from one to another only to find the right one after Sugarbaker had already checked out.

I was halfway through town, past the spot where Jenny McElvey was sketching a man in his early forties, when I recalled the motel Sugarbaker had mentioned, the one that Wescott told him was too far for him to drive to—the Winding Road Inn. For that I would need my truck.

The Winding Road Inn was several miles outside of town. It was ten-thirty by the time I got there. I pulled into the lot and parked next to a county car.

The motel was a brown-shingled building with a dining room and bar in the middle and wings on either side. I walked in past the salad bar to the registration desk on the right. On the far side of the salad bar I could see customers at the tables. A number looked like the women I had breakfasted with. I recalled now that I had heard this was a popular spot during Bohemian Week. I wondered if David Sugarbaker had heard that too.

"What room is David Sugarbaker in?" I asked the desk clerk.

"One-eleven." He surveyed me top to bottom, sweater to jeans. His expression, as he pointed to the corridor behind him, said that tastes vary.

I could have had the desk clerk call Sugarbaker and ask him to meet me at the restaurant instead of charging along to his room. But I only needed to know what Alison had been doing at the bar and how long she was doing it. That would take two minutes. If I waited for him to get himself in shape to face breakfast, I might have to wait until noon.

I knocked on the door of room 111. There was no answer. Surely he hadn't gone out. He should have

been in no shape to go anywhere this morning. I
knocked again.

It was on the fifth knock (loud enough that the
man across the hall looked out) that Sugarbaker
pulled the door open. I had expected him to be hung
over, but he was beyond that. He looked barely hu-
man. His sandy hair hung down over his forehead in
oily clumps. His eyelids were puffy and his eyes
barely visible. His color was appropriate for one
who deals with cesspools.

"Did I get you up?" I asked.

"I should be so lucky." He made his way back to
the bed, pulling his maroon cotton bathrobe tighter
around him and trying to re-tie the belt. "Alcohol
keeps me awake. I manage to forget that while I'm
drinking. I don't remember till I climb into bed.
Then I collapse and in half an hour I wake up sweating and spend the rest of the night thinking how
lousy I feel, and how lousy I'm going to feel."

I stood for a moment, again amazed at how he
could look so wasted and sound so lucid. Then I
propped all four pillows behind him. "Lie back
against these." Picking up the phone, I asked for
room service and ordered a large tomato juice with
lots of Worcestershire sauce, a piece of dry grain
bread, and a mix of egg yolk, salmon, and spinach,
steamed.

"Yuck," Sugarbaker managed to get out.

"Trust me. I used to be an account executive.
Dealing with hangovers is ground-floor knowledge.
I could explain what each ingredient is for—"

"Spare me that at least." He sprawled back
against the pillows. A moan flowed from his mouth
as a consequence of the movement.

I pulled the one padded chair over and sat. "Last

night you were telling me about Michelle Davidson. . . ."

His eyes opened slightly. He stared at me. "Oh,
you're the one in the bar."

I was tempted to ask who he thought I was, but
most likely he hadn't thought at all.

"Right. Did Michelle seem nervous, or frightened,
or worried?"

His eyes returned to their nearly closed position. I
couldn't tell whether he was considering his answer
or going to sleep. Finally, he said, "No."

"Not worried, or nervous, or frightened?"

"Just teed off. She just wanted to know about her
larvae." He pushed himself up, propped himself on
his elbow, and focused his barely opened eyes on
me. "I told her how things work. See there was no
perk test done of that property and that—"

"What's a perk test?"

"Perk tests test the soil, its ability to handle water
coming into it—how the water percolates into it."

"Oh, and then how much it would absorb the
water from the cesspool?"

"Right. But they've only been required for the last
few years. Before that you could put a cesspool on
cement and no one would care."

I didn't see that the absorption of the soil was
likely to affect Michelle's death. "What else did you
talk about?"

"I told her what a cesspool is. It's just a redwood
box. A lot of people, even people who grew up with
them, don't know that. It's usually about four-by-
six. The outlet pipe that leads to the leach lines is
high enough so that only the water and the bacteria
flow out."

"The bacteria goes into the soil?" I asked, appalled.

His cheeks moved with the hint of a smile. "A lot of people are shocked. We've even had people go out and dig up their vegetable gardens and throw everything out."

I could understand that.

"The bacteria in the soil eats the bacteria in the effluent. By the time the water penetrates the soil it's sterile."

"I'll take your word for that."

"A lot of people are skeptical. They don't know the first thing about containers. Some people think that they have to change their cesspools every year, and other people expect one redwood box to last a lifetime."

"How long should one last?"

"Thirty years, given normal use. Of course, you move in eight or ten people and you're going to fill up sooner."

I thought of Ward McElvey's cesspool. His father-in-law had been digging the hole for it when he died. That was eight years ago. I asked, "Did Michelle mention that her neighbor's cesspool was only eight years old?"

"Oh, yeah. I told her that was real odd. Those people must either have had lots of guests or terrible bowels." Again there was the hint of a smile. I assumed intestinal humor came with the job at Environmental Health. "They should have had a perk test done before they put it in. Some soil just won't percolate enough."

"But everyone else on that block has cesspools or septic tanks and they're not overrunning their leach lines."

"A lot of people think that way." He nodded di- dactically. "But soil isn't the same from one yard to the next. One place you've got a spring, another place a hidden rock formation. It's nothing for an amateur to deal with."

It was already more than I wanted to know.

"Michelle was real interested. She understood."

There was a knock on the door. I opened it and told the boy to put the tray on the bed.

No longer supported by the stimulation of sew- age, Sugarbaker slumped back against the pillows.

I tipped the boy.

"Sit up," I said to Sugarbaker. "How's your head?"

"Three sizes too small for my brain."

I took a bottle of Tylenol from my purse. "Take two with your juice." I put the glass in one of his hands and the pills in the other. "Take a drink first."

He sniffed the Worcestershire-heavy juice. "Yuck."

"Don't talk, drink."

He sipped tentatively then downed the pills. His eyes opened.

It occurred to me that this was the first time I'd really seen his eyes. They were brown. I took the glass and handed him the plate.

He looked down. His mouth started to form a "Yuck" but he caught himself before he said it. With the same amount of belief that I had had in the soil bacteria eating the effluent bacteria, he looked at the salmon, spinach, and yolk mixture that sat atop the grain bread. He forked a tiny bite and chewed as if every move of his jaw hurt. Staring down at his plate, he said, "This looks like it's been eaten be- fore."

"Beauty is only skin deep."

He forked another bite.

"You remember the woman you saw at the bar—the woman with the overalls and the wild blond hair?"

He continued to chew. "Yeah, the one Michelle got so mad about."

"What was she doing there, in the bar?"

He took another swallow of juice. His brow scrunched. He stared at me. "Hey, you were with that jerk of a sheriff, weren't you? I remember now. They told me that after you left. Made me feel like a real fool. I thought you helped me, but you didn't. You were with him."

"It was a mistake. I'm sorry. I thought you were someone else."

"Big deal. Sorry! That didn't stop that jerk from dragging me outside."

"I'm sorry. If I'd known—"

"And then you walked out on me."

"You were drunk. You do remember that."

"And now you barge in here when I feel like hell."

"And I give you medicine and get you breakfast."

"Just get out."

I hesitated. I'd already been thrown out once this morning. But I needed to know about Alison. "Tell me about the woman at the bar first."

"I'm not telling you another thing."

But I had one more bit of leverage. "That county car in the lot, that's yours, right? It's easy to check. You brought it here Thursday, right? It's going to be hard enough for you to explain why you've still got it Saturday morning. I'm sure Environmental Health doesn't work on weekends, not checking mosquito larvae."

"I have other inspections here."

"Saturday inspections?"

"Listen—"

"I'm also sure you don't want Environmental Health to know you were driving the county car after the sheriff told you you were too drunk to get behind the wheel."

"Damn you!"

"The woman in the bar. How long was she there?"

He sat clutching his plate. Briefly I wondered if he might throw it like Craig had the vase. Finally he said, "Not long. She only came in to buy a bottle of wine. That doesn't take more than five minutes."

"You saw her come and go?"

"Come and go," he repeated.

"One more thing," I said.

"Why not?"

"I saw you in Michelle's yard yesterday morning and in the afternoon about four. You were looking down toward the sewer hole where the sheriff and Michelle's husband and I were standing. If you'd already checked the garage, what were you doing there?"

"Can't you guess?"

"Tell me."

"I thought she'd be home. I didn't expect her husband—"

"After she walked out of the bar?"

"Well, things seem different in daylight. We'd gotten along pretty well. She's a real looker. I thought I'd tell her I'd come to do a view test of the soil, nothing real scientific, just eyeballing it."

"Why did you leave all of a sudden?"

"Like you said, I saw the sheriff and a man. The

man looked like he lived there. I didn't want to find out."

"And you'd parked up the hill on the next street, right?"

"Yeah. I didn't want to leave my car parked in front." He took another bite of the salmon mixture. He seemed to have forgotten he was mad at me. "We got along real well, Michelle and me. She dug me, I could tell." His brow scrunched again. He stared at me. "Hey, you said you were there. You and your friend the sheriff. What were you doing there? Meeting a woman isn't illegal."

"Michelle's dead. They'd just taken her body out of the sewer hole."

In one movement he flung the plate aside, clutched his mouth, and ran for the bathroom.

So Alison had not been with Craig, slaving over the books all Thursday evening. She had been at the bar, albeit briefly. She'd been buying a bottle of wine. Was it to take back to the plant shop? I doubted it. If she'd bought a couple of beers I could accept that. A beer is what you'd want after hauling plants around the shop floor or going over the books till ten. You'd be hot, tired, anxious for a long cold drink. You wouldn't want a sip of Chablis.

No, a bottle of wine is what Alison would buy for a client's rendezvous. Wine was certainly easy to come by here, in Sonoma County, the wine country. But you couldn't go to an empty house for a rendezvous and call out for it as if you were ordering pizza. Getting it there was the Bohemian Connection's job.

Everything pointed to Alison as the Connection. She was the person Ross had stayed with. She knew his failings and still allowed him to live with her. He had brought her to Henderson during Bohemian Week when she could meet whomever she would need to know. She was strong, competent, and able to look after herself.

I needed to talk to Alison. Normally she would be in the shop, but that was closed. I knew where she lived—a boardinghouse on the block behind the PG&E office here in town. It was an old three-story clapboard building that looked like a transplanted

Boston rowhouse—an undecorated rectangle chopped off at the property lines, and stark in spite of the eucalyptus trees and wild blackberry vines that filled the lot on either side. I had read the meter there often enough to have a sense of how small the rooms were. It was definitely not a place Alison would choose to spend a free Saturday afternoon.

And, after working all week with plants, I was willing to bet that the place that would appeal to Alison now would be bare of even grass—the beach.

An access road sloped down from North Bank Road to the beach. The pavement ended, and cars parked against the bank and in two rows between there and the concession stand. Beyond the stand the beach was filled with sunbathers. There were no parking spots left by this time, almost noon. I pulled up next to the concession stand and parked along the rear wall, hoping that I would be quick enough to avoid the sheriff's patrol. That was one group I didn't expect any special favors from.

I took off my shoes and rolled up the legs of my jeans. The beach was only about fifty yards wide. It was ample for a town the size of Henderson, and swamped by twice as many tourists. Making my way between blankets, chairs, and coolers required considerable concentration. Straight ahead were the beached canoes waiting to be rented. There were only five now, but by evening there would be ten times that number. Further out in the water a wooden raft rode low under the weight of children, swaying as they climbed on and tipping precariously close to the water line when they dove off.

I made my way to the west side of the beach near the summer dam. It was the dam that the town put in each summer to make the water deep enough to swim in. It was the same dam that had caught Ross's mother's body after her suicide. Alison lay on a blanket at the farthest point of the beach, almost in the parking area. She was wearing a shiny red bikini and lying on a yellow- and black-striped blanket. Her hair spread out from her head like ripples of corn-blond water.

The blanket was loud, the bathing suit skimpy for someone with a workman's tan like hers, but on Alison it looked right, as if her pale shoulders and stomach only served to contrast with the bright red of the suit. Surveying the beach, I realized that Alison's was the one blanket that stood out. Was that because of her natural stylishness or was it calculated to make it easier for those seeking the Bohemian Connection?

I made my way around two full-sized army blankets and waited while a family of grandparents, parents, aunts, and six children of various ages trooped in front of me to the river.

As I came to Alison's blanket, she opened her eyes. She looked like a different person than the stylish woman who had been at Vida's potluck dinner a few months ago, or even the woman who was working in the yard on Route 116 yesterday. She looked like a tired, older person. There were dark circles under her eyes and her hand shook as she reached for her sunglasses.

"You look exhausted," I said.

"I didn't get much sleep. It hasn't been, well, it's been pretty depressing at the shop."

"I can imagine."

"Craig's not good at handling something like death," she went on. "The Sheriff's Department still has Michelle's body. It's in a funeral home. Did you know we don't have a morgue in Sonoma County? Isn't that amazing. I thought any place as large as Santa Rosa would have a morgue."

"Is the coroner doing tests?"

"What?"

"On the body." I couldn't bring myself to refer to the body that was being cut up and analyzed as Michelle.

"Oh. I don't know. Craig didn't say. He just can't plan for the funeral and he doesn't know what to do." Alison looked to be in the same shape. She stood up, reached down for a corner of the blanket and picked it up, holding it out as if she didn't know how it had gotten in her hand. "I thought I'd sleep in the sun. But I wasn't sleeping."

Had she been up all night worrying about Craig? It wasn't the response I would have expected from cool, controlled Alison. I could more easily believe she had been delivering marijuana or cocaine to errant chairmen of the board.

"Alison," I said, "do you remember telling me that Ross brought you up here one weekend?"

She nodded.

"When was that?"

If the abruptness of the question surprised her, she didn't show it. She looked down at the blanket hanging from her hand. "It was just this time of year. I remember that because there was a party at Jim's bar on a Saturday night. It was called the Bohemian Ball—the first and last, I understand. Jim thought it would be fun for the townspeople to have their own Bohemian festivities, so he arranged that. People were supposed to come dressed as bohemians, however they chose to define that. They may have come that way, but they left as drunks. By the time Ross and I cleared out the sheriff had been there four times and left with a carload three of those times."

"What year was that?"

She shook the blanket and began folding it. "Not recent."

"How not recent?"

"Not in the last couple of years."

"Can you be more specific?"

She stood staring down at the blanket. "No. I can't. I don't have much of a sense of long-term time. I'm real reliable on what I have to do this week, maybe even this month. But I don't think about the past much and it all runs together."

"But surely—"

"No, believe me, Vejay. I've been through this type of thing before."

"Okay then, on the more recent scene, you were in the bar Thursday night about ten, buying a bottle of wine. How come?"

For the first time she looked alert. She stopped with the blanket half-folded and stared at me. Then she continued to fold in silence.

"Craig told me you were never out of the shop that night. Why would he say that?"

"It was only ten minutes. He probably forgot." She started toward the cars. "Did Michelle's aunt put you up to asking that, Vejay? Because if she did—"

"Good weekend for some fun, eh girls?" Two men stood in our path. I had been so absorbed in my questions I hadn't heard their footsteps. Alison almost walked into them. The speaker, a man of about fifty with styled hair and tan slacks, looked us over appraisingly and let his gaze come to rest on

Alison. His companion, somewhat younger, but similarly dressed, watched nervously.

"How about a drink?" the spokesman asked.

When a similar offer had been made to Vida and me last year it took me a few minutes to realize that during Bohemian Week any two youngish women together were likely to be mistaken for hookers. Vida hadn't been so slow on the uptake. Now I watched how Alison handled this.

"No," she said in the same tired voice. "I'm on my way to work." She looked past me. "And Vejay has to leave in a hurry." She pointed to my truck, which the sheriff was inspecting.

I raced over through the sand. Sheriff Wescott was pulling out his pad. When he saw me his face reset into a scowl.

With a sigh, I said, "I suppose I can't convince you that I was just here a moment."

"Nothing personal," he said in an all-business tone. "Time isn't the issue. It's not a parking spot."

"Look, I'm sorry about last night. I would have called to tell you that, but there wasn't anything I could say. I figured the best thing I could do was to stay out of your way."

"Do you have a driver's license?"

I extricated it from my wallet and held it out.

"Take it out of the plastic case, please."

I did. "I realized it was an embarrassing mistake, but Sugarbaker does look a lot like Ross Remson. Even Michelle told him so."

He stopped, pen poised, and stared at me in disgust. "You talked to him after that?" In the bright sun, in his brown uniform, against the background of the sand, he looked all tan—weatherworn and hard.

"I needed to know why Michelle met him Thursday night."

"Registration?"

"Look—"

"Registration."

I climbed into the cab, opened the glove compartment, and pulled out the papers—owner's manual, repair record, maps of California, San Francisco, Sonoma and Marin Counties, and the registration.

"You've made your point," I said. "I've told you I'm sorry. I wish I could do something to make you less angry, but there apparently isn't anything that would do that."

He handed back the registration, then continued to write out the ticket.

When he held out my copy, I took it and said, "Just one question, an innocuous one."

He didn't speak, but he didn't turn away either.

"Do you remember a Bohemian Ball held at the bar some years ago?" The weekend Ross brought Alison to Henderson.

"It was before my time."

"When exactly was it?"

"I'm not even going to ask why you want to know that."

"And you're not going to answer me?"

"I did."

I climbed into the cab of my pickup and carefully shut the door. I wasn't about to give Sheriff Wescott the satisfaction of seeing how furious I was. I pulled slowly away from the concession stand and drove in first gear around the parked cars behind the beach. So intent was I on preserving my image that I missed the exit road nearest my house, and since I was hardly about to circle past the concession stand— and Sheriff Wescott—again, I had to take the far exit to Zeus Lane.

It wasn't till I reached the intersection at North Bank Road and sat vainly watching for a break in the bumper-to-bumper traffic on the main road that I realized the sheriff didn't need to see a driver's license, much less a registration, to write out a parking ticket!

"Damn him!"

I yanked the steering wheel to the left, ready to make a U-turn and barrel back down to the beach. But an ice cream truck sat inches from my back bumper and there wasn't room to pull forward and make the turn. And by now Wescott was probably gone anyway. He was probably driving away from the beach in his official car, laughing.

So I sat, watching the traffic and feeling the sweat drip down my back. Any suggestion of the morning fog had long gone. There was no breeze. The sun reflected off the roadway, and the open windows of my pickup only provided an entryway for the heat.

During the noon hour of the first Saturday of Bohemian Week I should have known North Bank Road would be jammed. Limousines with their tinted windows inched along toward the turn-off for the Bohemian Grove. Occasionally a carefully coiffed head of white hair would be visible in a back seat. Interspersed throughout the general flow were the Mercedes of the younger rich who still drove themselves, and the station wagons of the tourist families heading toward their motels or the ocean.

Across North Bank Road was the empty parking lot of Davidson's Plants. Catching staccato glimpses of it between the passing trucks, I noticed that even the shop truck was gone.

Two ancient school buses labeled HOLINESS CHRISTIAN DAY SCHOOL passed. Three small hands waved out the windows. I waved back. An equally ancient pickup pulled into the Davidson's Plants parking lot. A man climbed out and stalked up to the closed door of the shop. Even from across the street I could see how filthy his jeans and workshirt were.

A Volkswagen van stopped in the intersection, blocking my line of vision. When it moved, I could see the man banging on the glass door of the plant shop. His matted beard and long hair shook stiffly with each hit. But the door remained closed. Apparently Craig had learned from his mistake of letting me in this morning.

I inched the pickup forward. Two limousines crossed the intersection.

The man was still there, still banging, still eliciting no response. Finally he stopped, turned toward North Bank Road, and stood considering.

Seeing him full on, I recognized him. He was the man who had bought the African violet from Craig yesterday. Had he taken it home to a wife who told him what a sorry plant it was? Had she sent him back to replace it with a healthy one?

To my left, in the eastbound lane, a Mercury hesitated. I jutted the nose of my pickup forward, blocking the lane. But the westbound, beach- and Grovebound vehicles kept moving.

Over in Davidson's lot, the man climbed back into his truck.

To my left, drivers began to honk their horns.

The man pulled out of Davidson's lot toward North Bank Road.

I punched a long blast on my own horn. A westbound station wagon paused. I shot across. The man from Craig's lot turned right into the westbound traffic—into the space I'd created.

Momentarily, I considered pulling into the plant shop lot and turning around to follow him. But I knew that would be futile. By the time someone let me into the line of traffic, he would be halfway to Jenner. Instead, I drove on, making a right onto the street that paralleled North Bank Road, and headed to the PG&E office.

The gate to the lot was closed, but my key was on my ring. I unlocked it and pulled in, leaving my truck behind one of the utility pickups we used when reading meters. The larger trucks, the trouble trucks, driven by the trouble men who handled customer's complaints, were parked against the building. I unlocked the office door and walked into the cool darkness of the meter readers/supply room.

Even for an empty building the office seemed oddly quiet this Saturday, like a room where someone has died. I had worked Saturdays before; we all had occasionally. It wasn't a matter of choice. But on those days the office, without the clerks and the customers, was only slightly different than it was on weekdays. It had the feel of the last day before Christmas holidays. Then, those of us who had to work waited in the office till everyone was in and we could head for the bar. Of course, then I was paid to be here. Today, I had no legitimate reason.

The walls of the meter readers' room were painted the same tan as the trucks. The metal bookcases were tan, the old wooden table in the center of the room might once have been another color, but if so, the paint had worn off over the years, leaving bare, worn wood that was, of course, tan. And in the corner was the San Francisco bag. After the initial coolness of the dark room, it now seemed warm and close. Nothing moved. There was no sound except for my movements and a steady whirr coming from the center of the building.

The route books were on a lazy Susan. HE6 (Henderson, Route 6) was in front. I pulled it out and opened it near the end, then flipped back through the pages until I found Maria Keneally's page. Under her name and address were directions to her meter. And there was space for comments, warnings such as "lawn mushy" or "occupant hostile" or "Doberman hides behind house." For Maria Keneally it read, "offers tea."

On the opposite page was what I sought—a listing of her usage for the past two years. Maria Keneally had been in the hospital and then recuperated with a relative in San Rafael last winter. As with this year's vacation, the hospitalization had been planned. She had discussed turning off all her appliances with me.

And indeed for January there was no usage at all recorded. I glanced at the figures for the last read period, most of June and a week of July. They should have been the same as January.

But they weren't. The usage was minimal, but there was usage. It was a small enough amount that had the house belonged to someone else, someone with whom I hadn't discussed the preparations for departure, I would have assumed that a neighbor was coming in and leaving a light on. But Maria Keneally hadn't had anyone check on her house in January when nights came early and an unlit house was a clear target for our winter burglars. She certainly wouldn't worry during the short nights of summer. Besides, I recalled how pleased she had been to get her first bill in February and find $0.00 on it. She had saved it to show me.

But there would be no zero this time. The usage listed for the past month was before Bohemian Week. It would be more this month. I wondered how frequently the Bohemian Connection used Miss Keneally's house. It was secluded and yet easy to get to. For a rendezvous it was almost too appealing to pass up.

"Miss Haskell! What are you doing here?"

Dropping the book on the table, I spun around. "Mr. Bobbs, what are *you* doing here on Saturday?"

"Working. But this is not a work weekend for you."

I couldn't tell him I was checking the PG&E records to confirm a suspicion that had nothing to do with my job. That it related to a murder would make it only more suspect. Trying to think as Mr. Bobbs would, I said, "One of the reads was bothering me. I had to see if I'd recorded it right. I was afraid I'd transposed the numbers."

Anyone else would have asked if it couldn't have waited till Monday. But Mr. Bobbs hesitated. Coming in on a day off to check a read was clearly not a preposterous idea to him. Finally he said, "And did you?"

"Transpose the numbers? No, I had it right." I closed the route book and put it back on the lazy Susan. As I lifted my arms I felt a cool breeze on my back. I realized the whirr was louder.

Mr. Bobbs still stared suspiciously. His thin brown hair clung to his scalp. In spite of the closeness in the building he wore his tan jacket. The only concession to the heat he'd made was to unbutton the top button of his shirt. I wondered if he had been sitting alone in his office, thusly dressed, or if he'd put on his jacket before coming out to see who was skulking in the back room.

"Miss Haskell, it is against policy to enter the office on off days for any reason. We do have—"

"I didn't want a mistake to go unnoticed. When you're only allowed three mistakes per thousand reads, you can't be too careful." My reads had always been under the error limit, but this was still not a topic I wanted to discuss with Mr. Bobbs. To divert him, I asked, "Was it my suggestion that you were considering here on a Saturday?"

His round face looked blank for a moment. I walked through the doorway into the center room where the clerks sat. A counter separated it from the lobby area where customers came to pay their bills, or to question them. To the left was Mr. Bobbs's cubicle. From it I could feel the cold air, and hear the whirr of an air conditioner—his portable air conditioner that he never brought to the office when we meter readers were around. Vaguely I recalled a memo telling us that personal appliances were not allowed.

He moved around me with more agility than I would have imagined possible and stood in his doorway.

I controlled a smile. "My suggestion? Is that what you're working on today?"

He stepped to one side of the doorway, blocking my view of his air conditioner. "Miss Haskell, as I have told you on each of the many occasions you have asked about this, your suggestion is in Followup."

"For what date?"

"For a time when I can give it my uninterrupted attention."

Pointedly, I glanced around the empty office.

His neck muscles tightened; his neck looked very red and rough against the soft tan of his collar. "When I put your suggestion in Follow-up, I dated it for the day that would be most advantageous for it —when it will get my best attention."

"When it will be most convenient for you," I almost said. But as he moved again to block the view of the illicit energy-gobbling air conditioner, I could see his desk. On it was a copy of the *Utility Reporter,* the union paper. Suddenly I felt sad. Mr. Bobbs had come to the office on his day off to covertly read our union paper. Where could he live, what could his life be like that he would find it preferable to come to this closed-up building on a Saturday afternoon? The idea to invite him out for a beer flickered through my mind. I dismissed it. I had distressed him enough for one day. Having a beer with me was probably what he would view as atonement for a mortal sin.

"See you Monday," I said, and headed for the back door. Mr. Bobbs walked as far as the supply room entry. As I closed the door I could see him heading toward the routebooks to check what I had taken or left.

I headed through town toward Half Hill Road. Maria Keneally's house was more important than I had realized. Someone was in there using electricity. Alison had been there yesterday. I would have to find out what she was doing there. If she was the Bohemian Connection she wasn't going to tell me. I would have to watch the house when the Bohemian Connection brought clients there—at night. Tonight. But not until tonight. Maybe something would happen before then to make that unnecessary.

Meanwhile, I'd have to content myself with checking in with Vida. It was a safe bet that she would be at Craig's house.

North Bank Road was still crowded, but not nearly as bad as before. A group licking ice cream cones crossed in front of me, reminding me that it was one o'clock and I hadn't had lunch. But even for someone of my considerable appetite, the hassle of looking for a parking spot downtown was more than hunger could justify. I drove on.

I glanced at Jenny McElvey as I glided past in first gear. She was just tearing off a sketch and handing it to a man. At the corner I turned right, drove past the closed nursery and on up to Half Hill Road.

I was still pondering my run-in with Mr. Bobbs as I pulled up next to the sewer hole. I'll bet he'd like to have that to chuck Follow-up suggestions in, I thought. And then with a clutch of guilt I remembered Michelle's body in that hole, and how sepulchral that hole had been.

I climbed down from the cab of my truck and walked around the far side of the hole.

Vida came down the stairs from Michelle's house. She was wearing a maroon dress, hot for a day like this. She had on high heels and carried a purse. Her face looked even more lined and tired than it had yesterday.

"Oh, Vejay," she said. "I'm just on my way to the funeral home."

I nodded.

She started to walk on, then stopped. "It's just so awful, Vejay. The sheriff's still holding Michelle's body. He won't say when he'll release it. We can't set a time for the funeral. We don't know when it will be. Craig's falling apart. He couldn't handle making funeral arrangements at all. He hasn't even been near the house all day. He's holed up in his shop. I guess it's best for him to be working. But the kids are still in Santa Rosa; they've got to be told some time. I don't know when Craig will be up to that. And there are Michelle's clothes. . . . Oh, Vejay, I just can't believe she's really dead."

I squeezed her hand and waited till her sobs stopped. "I was just in the office looking up something when Mr. Bobbs sneaked up on me," I said, mostly to fill the silence. "He'd been at his desk. And guess what he has there?"

Vida looked up.

"An illicit air conditioner! He must sneak in on Saturdays and use the company's power."

Vida's mouth wavered a moment, then she smiled.

"Well, we all have our vices. But what were *you* doing there on Saturday?"

"I wanted to check the usage for a house I think the Bohemian Connection is using. Mr. Bobbs caught me with the routebook open. But I fended him off with a question about my Follow-up suggestion."

Vida moved a foot forward as if easing into departure.

"The thing is, Vida, I'm sure the Bohemian Connection has something to do with Michelle's murder."

Her hand tightened on her purse. "Vejay, I'm too upset to think about that. To be honest, I'm sorry I ever called you—not that you haven't really put yourself out, I don't mean that, I know you have. But now the sheriff won't give us Michelle's body. I wish she had just died with nothing questionable about it."

"But she didn't. I'm sorry about the added misery this is to you, but it's too late to change that. Maybe you'll feel better when you know what I've figured out."

She didn't respond, but she didn't leave either.

"When Ross Remson left, the Bohemian Connection passed on to his successor. That successor, if it wasn't Michelle herself, was someone she knew. She was the one person in Henderson who cared about Ross, the one person he was likely to tell. So she was a danger to the present Connection."

Vida put a hand on my arm. "Vejay, it's bad enough she died in the sewer without dragging her name into an operation as seamy as that. If that's what you're thinking, just leave the whole thing alone."

I took a breath. "I'm only telling *you* this. I'm not broadcasting it. But look, killing her was one thing, but putting her body down that hole was another. Why would someone do that? I mean, it's not like burying it miles away where no one would find it. This was a very temporary arrangement. If her body wasn't discovered by someone like me over the weekend, then it would have been found first thing Monday morning when the sewer construction crew arrived. It's like Follow-up. The killer just put her body there to keep it out of the way for a while."

"But why?"

"That is the question. What would anyone gain by hiding Michelle's body for three days? If the killer had left town and used those three days to put distance between himself and Henderson it would have made sense. But everyone involved with Michelle and the Bohemian Connection was still here."

Vida stared at the hole, her fingers pressing even tighter against her purse. "Maybe the killer wanted to prevent Michelle from doing something?"

"Okay. But it would have had to have been something that she was going to do this weekend. He kept her from doing it, but also tried to avoid the publicity of her death—at least until Monday. What is it that Michelle was going to do?"

With a sigh, Vida said, "Demonstrate. She was going to picket outside the Grove."

"Which brings us back to the Bohemian Connection."

"Not necessarily. She could have been killed by a pimp. Some guy—"

"You don't really think that, do you, Vida?"

It was a moment before she shook her head. "No.

We've never had any trouble with any of them here."

"Was there anything else Michelle planned for this weekend?"

Vida looked back at the sewer hole. She was silent for a full minute. "No, nothing she didn't do any other weekend."

The sun was hot on my hair; my T-shirt stuck to my back. There seemed to be an odd odor coming from the direction of the sewer hole—an odor of decay. But the odor was in my mind; Michelle's body was gone. I had seen it carried out. I'd been down in the hole after it was gone. I'd climbed up; the sheriff had seen me, and Craig, and Sugarbaker. Sugarbaker!

"There was something else Michelle was going to do this weekend, Vida. She was going to talk to her congressman. She was going to ask him about speeding up action on her cesspool complaint."

Vida smiled. "I can see Michelle doing that. I can see her striding up to the platform and demanding his attention. But, Vejay, if she wasn't killed because she was going to demonstrate, she surely wasn't murdered because she complained about mosquito larvae."

"I suppose. But I think we should tell the congressman when he's here."

"No." Her teeth clamped together. I'd seen that "don't push me" look before when Vida chaired the union meetings. "There's a limit. We've had enough publicity in this family."

"I'll do it. You won't have to be involved."

"Vejay, just let it go, will you? I don't want to hear theories; I don't want to talk about Bohemians. I have to look at caskets and try to make some arrangements. It will be a big funeral." She walked toward her truck.

"Just one thing," I said as she was about to climb in. "Do you remember a Bohemian Ball at the bar some years ago?"

"Vejay, I said no more."

I caught her arm. "You asked me to find out about Michelle. I've done nothing else since noon yesterday. I've annoyed people I barely knew, I've made an enemy of the sheriff, and I've been physically attacked. It's too late for you to withdraw your request. You owe me, at least enough to answer my question."

Vida took a step back, freeing her arm. From the look on her face it wasn't clear if she was stunned or angry.

"Vida."

"All right. I do owe you an answer. Yes, I do recall the Bohemian Ball."

"When was it?"

She opened the door to her pickup and stood with one foot on the rise, teetering slightly in her high heels. "I remember that. It was a big thing, with the costumes and all. People were getting pushed out of shape by the Bohemians coming in and partying then. There was a lot of jealousy here. Jim picked up on that. He's very good at sensing things before they get out of hand. So he arranged the First Annual Bohemian Ball. Or, he thought it would be the first."

"I gather it ended poorly."

"Like so many things here. Too much liquor. Jim was too new to the area then to sense that coming. But still, it was a good idea. People put a lot of thought into their costumes. I remember that because Michelle wanted to go. She was so disappointed and angry when she couldn't. She carried on for days."

"Didn't she have a date?"

"Michelle always had dates. She was going with Craig then. But the Bohemian Ball was in the bar. Michelle wasn't old enough. She was still a month short of turning eighteen." Vida climbed into the truck and quickly shut the door. "I'm really late." She started the engine.

I backed away. As I watched the truck's departure, I spotted a fellow onlooker—Ward McElvey. He was sitting on his steps beside the garage. He looked as if he'd been sitting there in the sun for some time. His light blue shirt was blotched with sweat; sweat outlined his underarms and streaked down the middle of his chest. His polyester pants stuck to his legs. And his hair, which had been fluffed with a dryer when I last saw him, now hung limp.

I made my way around the sewer hole to him and asked, "Are you waiting for someone?"

"Jenny. I told her to be here at one o'clock. I have things to do, people to see. This is a busy time for real estate." He glared at his watch. "It's nearly one-thirty."

It was more like quarter after. "And you've been sitting in the sun waiting all this time?"

"Yeah."

"Is your other car in the garage?"

"Other car? There is no other car. What we have is the Pacer, and Jenny took that."

"But you dropped her off. I saw you unloading this morning."

He glared at me. "Well, that was then. I figured that I could take her and all her paraphernalia downtown and leave her for the day. I had to wait half an hour after I planned to leave to do it. I had to rearrange an appointment. Was she thankful? You bet she wasn't," he said without waiting for a response. "Then, I'm not in the office an hour before she calls. She's got to have the car. Her easel broke and she's got to get it fixed."

"Why didn't she go to Gresham's? Surely they could tape up an easel at the hardware store."

"Ask her, if she deigns to drop by. She seems to think the only place that can deal with the complicated equipment of the finer art world is on the road to Santa Rosa." He glared at his watch again. "I don't know why I married into that bunch of loonies. One's worse than the next. The best of the lot was old Mrs. Remson."

"Why?"

"Because she had the decency to drown herself."

I expected him to look up in embarrassment, to back off from his statement. He didn't.

I sat next to him on the step. I wanted to ask him about Alison and if she had had any professional contact with him.

"Single-minded, that's what they are. With Jenny, it's her art. The earthquake could come and she wouldn't notice, unless she thought the rubble would be suitable for a still life. Have you seen the inside of our house? It's like an art museum. You can't find the plaster for the paintings. You know . . ." He looked at me as if just realizing I was there. "What's your name?"

"Vejay."

"You know, Vejay, I don't like the paintings. I never told her that, of course, but those canvases are like . . ." He searched for the right word. "They're like wounds on the wall. You can't see the house for the paintings."

I sat still, amazed by this outburst.

But Ward McElvey wasn't through. He took a breath. "Jenny couldn't hold a job, not a real job. She can't even stay down there on the sidewalk all day. If it's not her easel, it's her charcoal, or her lights, or something she needs at the house, or something she needs from Santa Rosa. She can't do anything that requires responsibility. She doesn't cook. She doesn't clean. Most of the time I doubt she knows I'm there. I'm just a convenience, someone to run the business and keep her in money. I've been a convenience to the whole goddamn Remson family. If they'd had to depend on Ross you know where they'd be? Down in that hole with Michelle, that's where. You couldn't count on him any more than on Jenny. Less. Always taking off whenever he felt like it. And even when he was here he was no use. You couldn't be sure he'd come to work. And when he was there it was all we could do, the old man and me, to make sure he stayed out of the way of the locals."

"Why was that?"

"Didn't trust him."

I took a guess. "Was that because he was the Bohemian Connection?"

"Yeah. This is a small town, you know . . ." He paused, looking at me, searching for my name, then gave up. "Like any little town there are two sets of rules, one for the outsiders and another for the locals. People don't care if tourists come in here and buy women and deal drugs. They don't object to anyone making a buck off the tourists; you can sell them whatever you like. But let me tell you, when it comes to dealing with the seller themselves, that's another story."

"You mean no one minded Ross being the Bohemian Connection, but they wouldn't want to buy a house from him."

"You got it, lady. Pain in the butt, too. The old man had to have him there. His son could do no wrong. I couldn't even suggest that he might possibly be hurting the business. Oh, no. Closest I could come was to say that he might do better with the out-of-town buyers. Old man bought that. He knew what was going on; he just didn't want to admit it. But I'll tell you, doing all the local work and sifting out newcomers for Ross—if he happened to be in—was no picnic."

"You must have been glad when he left."

"No loss, let me—"

The Pacer roared up the street and squealed to a halt inches from my truck. Jenny jumped out and hurried toward the house. She stopped abruptly in front of us. Had there been room on the stairs she would have rushed on into the house without pause.

"About time," Ward said.

"I couldn't leave." It was a statement rather than an apology.

"I needed the car at one o'clock."

"Why? Are you carting around your Sunset Villa guests?"

I'd forgotten about the Underwoods, the older couple Ward had been taking to the site of his senior citizen condominiums yesterday.

"They're gone," he said.

"Oh."

"They said it was too dangerous up here." Ward glared at the sewer hole.

Jenny laughed. "Maybe once they saw the site for Sunset Villas they decided they didn't want to live in an ark."

"What's that supposed to mean?"

"Come on, Ward, you know how far underwater that land will be when it floods."

"Sunset Villas will have foundations. There'll be stairs. The units aren't going to sit flat on the ground."

"Maybe they didn't want to travel from their door by canoe then."

Ward jumped up. For a moment I thought he was going to hit her. "Damn you. I do everything for you. Can't you ever think of me?"

She stepped back. A flicker of fear broke through her impassive expression. "I'm here, aren't I? It's not convenient. I had a subject waiting when I left." She glanced back at the car. "And the Pacer, Ward, you insisted on that car. We could have had two perfectly adequate used cars for what that cost. But you had to have that one. It's fine for driving around looking at houses. All that glass; it's made for looking. But it's no good for me. I can't leave anything in the car without wondering if it will be ripped off. If I put paints in the back they run. If I leave groceries, they spoil—"

"When do you deal with groceries?"

Looking at me, as Ward had, as if for the first time, Jenny said, "And have you come to watch us fight? It saves you the bother of asking questions, doesn't it?" Without waiting for a reply, she rushed past Ward up the stairs.

I expected him to follow her, but instead he sat back down. I expected him to apologize for their scene, to try to explain, at least to appear embarrassed. But he merely looked disgusted.

"About Alison," I said, realizing that Jenny could return any moment and Ward wouldn't be about to hang around to answer my questions then. "Did Alison ever ask you about rental properties?"

"Rental units? Hmm." He looked calmer as he considered his own area of interest. "She did, yes."

"Did she ask about ones with absentee landlords?"

"That's the only kind I handle. Local owners do their own renting."

"Did Alison ask where the owners live and if they come by often or at all?"

"That's right. She told me that they had a special service for landlords who couldn't come by to keep an eye on their property. They could assure them that it would be up to par. Seemed like a good thing."

"Did she ask specifically which landlords never came here at certain times of the year?" Another time Ward might have wondered what I was getting at, but his mind was still on his argument with Jenny. He was answering me on automatic pilot.

"She said she'd start with them."

"So you gave her their addresses?"

"Uh-huh."

The front door slammed.

"Did you take her to see the houses?"

Ward stood up. "No."

Jenny rushed down the stairs and past us to the car. Ward followed her. Hurrying after him, I said.

"Then did you give her the keys to look at the places herself?" It was a guess.

"Yes," he said as he jumped in the passenger's seat.

Suddenly I had a lot to consider and a lot of time to do it in. It was not quite two o'clock. It wouldn't be dark till nearly nine. There was nothing to do till then, except think.

And eat.

I headed back through town. The afternoon was still young. I could have a sandwich and then rent a canoe and paddle off some of the tension I had built up.

The drive along North Bank Road was slow. By habit I checked out Jenny's easel and chair; for once she was without a subject. Farther down the street I spotted Alison walking out of the bar—with the two men who'd come up to us on the beach! That was certainly something else to ponder.

At home I pulled my truck in by the garage, climbed out, and made my way up the stairs. A branch of poison oak was beginning to stick out between two steps. I'd need to put on gloves and work boots and climb under the stairs to uproot the plant. A project for another day.

I hurried on inside to the kitchen, made a chicken sandwich with cilantro, and took it and a glass of iced tea out onto my back porch. One of the bricks was coming loose from the back of the fireplace. I wondered if I could let that go and just continue losing a little heat in winter, or was a loose brick the

first warning of expensive disaster. Homeowning,
I'd discovered, had many surprises, few of them
pleasant, and none cheap.

It was just nine o'clock when I pulled my truck up
beside one of the cement pillars at the entrance to
the cemetery. Although I fully expected the Bohemian Connection to enter Maria Keneally's house
by way of the driveway, I felt it was tempting fate to
leave my truck in the cemetery parking area where it
could easily be seen.

It was getting chilly now. I didn't know how late
it would be before the Bohemian Connection arrived
with clients. Those clients might spend hours at one
of the bars before they chose to leave the bright
lights for the muted excitement of this rendezvous.
The Connection could drive up quietly and let them
in through the door that led off the garage. But I was
prepared. I had a blanket, a flashlight, a thermos of
coffee, and two sandwiches. I was wearing jeans, a
sweater and a down vest, and my work boots. I
found the other Maria Keneally's gravestone (from
where I could see the driveway) and settled atop it,
arranging my various belongings around me.

The living Maria Keneally's house was small.
From here I could see any light turned on in the
kitchen, bath, or bedroom, and the reflections of
lights from the living room and dining area. I was
tempted to circle the house, to make sure I hadn't
missed anything, but I vetoed that idea—no sense in
running into the Connection pulling up in the driveway.

So I sat. The wind was stronger at night. The big
redwoods rustled. Gusts blew fallen leaves against

the headstones. I draped the blanket over my shoulders.

I had had all day to ponder Michelle's murder but somehow I couldn't then. But now I considered her body in the sewer hole. Why had it been dropped down there? She had been murdered above ground. Why had her killer chosen to dump her body down there? As I had discussed with Vida, her murderer must have known Michelle's body would be found by Monday at the outside. It was late at night when he killed her—dark on Half Hill Road. He wouldn't have dumped the body down the hole because it was easy. It wouldn't have been easy. He would have had to have left the body slumped against the stairs, or against his car, then lifted the wooden cover off the sewer hole, carried the body back and thrown it in, then replaced the cover. Michelle was a small woman; it wouldn't have been hard to lift her body. But it all would have taken time. It would have made noise. Why hadn't the murderer chosen the easier way of simply sticking the body in his car and driving to some secluded place to drop it off. It was dark; the body would have been safe in any vehicle, even one as open as Ward McElvey's Pacer. There were plenty of spots around here to dump a body. It was not uncommon to read of bodies being discovered years after they disappeared.

And if the killer didn't want to leave Michelle's body in the woods, there was the Pacific Ocean half an hour away. If he'd dropped her body over one of the cliffs there would have been plenty of new bruises on it by the time it reached the ocean, and there would have been a chance of it being washed out to sea.

So why the sewer hole? Did the killer want the

body found? I pulled the blanket closer around my
shoulders. Why would the killer want the body
found? Was he trying to implicate someone else? I
couldn't imagine that. I was having enough trouble
believing any one of the people I knew had sufficient
reason to kill Michelle, without thinking that they
not only wanted her dead, but someone else impris-
oned.

Had Michelle been killed to avoid her picketing?
Everyone from Vida to the two prostitutes said that
was unlikely. Then had she been put out of the way
to keep her from talking to our congressman?

Forbes Tisson was a decent enough representative. An Independent, he appealed to the self-reliant
people of the Russian River area. But he seemed to
understand compromise and fitting in. I doubted
Forbes Tisson would go out of his way to rock the
boat. I could picture Michelle telling Tisson about
her mosquito larvae; I could see him assigning an
aide to look into that. I could see the aide dropping
a note to the Department of Environmental Health
and them sending David Sugarbaker (if he was still
on their payroll after this weekend's escapade with
the county car) out again. Maybe they would contact Ward McElvey. Maybe he would even have to
hook up to the sewer sooner than he wanted. Still,
Ward McElvey wouldn't be about to endanger his
home and business by killing a neighbor just to save
a thousand dollars.

So suppose Michelle had charged on and told Tisson about the prostitution problem? I almost
laughed. If Tisson would deal gingerly with the larvae, he would certainly do as little as possible to put
himself up against the powerful figures connected

with the Grove. At best he might make a statement condemning immorality.

So what I had here was the fact that Michelle's body had been thrown into the sewer hole, like Follow-up. And I had no idea why. Perhaps it would work itself out. Maybe I was going at it from the wrong end. Maybe I should just concentrate on Alison.

Had Michelle suspected her? There was no question about Michelle's feelings. And Craig? He had been angry as I questioned him, but when I asked about Alison, he had become enraged. Was he protecting her? Was she paying him off? Or was he her partner?

The wind was picking up, the air cooler. Even with the blanket on I was cold. I tried to see my watch, but it was too dark. I felt for the thermos and unscrewed the cap. As I tilted it to pour, the blanket fell off my shoulders. I vacillated between pouring and rewrapping, getting thoroughly cold before I made up my mind to go ahead and pour. And then I poured so fast that the coffee spilled over the edge and onto my jeans.

"Damn."

I put the cup down, recorked the thermos, screwed on the lid, pulled the blanket around me, and tried to pick up the cup without spilling any more. The gravestone didn't quite have the conveniences of home.

I sipped the coffee. And when I looked back at Maria Keneally's house, a light was on.

Either they had come with amazing stealth for people who had just left a bar, or I had been so overwhelmed with my coffee pouring that I'd missed them.

Putting the cup down and leaving the blanket, I picked up my flashlight and, stepping with exaggerated care on the leaves, circled around the side of the house, afraid I'd fooled around so long that the Connection would be gone and only the customers would remain.

But I was lucky. The Davidson's Plants truck was still in the driveway, and the garage door was partway up.

I made my way around the far side of the house, checking the windows as I went. They were too high for me to see in and all I could make out was light and shadows on the ceilings. As I suspected, the light was on only in the bedroom. I crept closer to the window, but I could make out no sounds of conversation. I moved around the corner by the other wall of the bedroom and next to the back door. Still I could hear nothing.

The light went off.

The back door opened.

I moved next to it.

A woman started out.

"What are you doing here, Alison?" I demanded.

She jumped back inside and pulled on the door, but I caught it before it closed, and wedged my work boot inside the door frame. I shoved the door back.

Alison turned abruptly, took a step toward the living room and the door that led to the garage.

"Stay where you are." I flicked the light switch on.

She stopped. In her arms were sheets and pillowcases.

I stood, waiting for her clients to come rushing from the bedroom, but there were no other sounds.

"Who's in there?" I asked.

"Where?"

"The bedroom."

"No one."

"Come on, I know what's going on."

Alison stared.

"I know you're the Bohemian Connection and you've got clients in that room."

Alison laughed. She let the sheets fall to the floor. "Is that what you think? High adventure here in Henderson? I wish I had a job as profitable as that."

I stayed by the door, ready to move fast. "Are you saying you're not the Bohemian Connection?"

"Right."

"You haven't brought a couple here for a rendezvous?"

"Right again."

"Then what are you doing breaking into an empty house on the first weekend of Bohemian Week?"

Alison pulled out one of the kitchen chairs and sat down with a thump. Her wild blond hair bounced, and absently she pushed a clump behind her ear. But she looked even more tired than she had today on the beach. She sighed. "Can't you guess why I'm here?"

I'd guessed enough. "Tell me."

"You were right to think this is a place for a rendezvous. It's perfect. I just came across it a month ago. And . . ." She looked away. It was the closest I'd seen Alison to looking embarrassed. "Craig and I—"

"Oh my god. You mean Michelle was right in her suspicions? You mean you and Craig were having an affair here?"

"It's not as tawdry as you make it sound," she said. "He couldn't come to my room in the rooming house, not without all of Henderson knowing. We could hardly use his house. He does have some standards. We couldn't go to a motel, not around here. Michelle knew too many people, and Craig was too easily recognized. There was nothing else, except the back of the truck, and that gets pretty hard after a while, to say nothing of lacking romance."

"So this is why you bought the bottle of wine at the bar Thursday night?"

She picked up one of the sheets and began fingering the edge. "Yes. We brought it up here. It was so nice, peaceful. I didn't realize it would be the last time."

"How come?"

"How come!" she snapped. "Craig felt guilty enough seeing another woman. He shouldn't have. Michelle was at him all the time. She didn't like the way he ran the shop; he didn't make enough money; he wasn't home enough; she had to do everything for the kids. She was the one who wanted the kids to begin with. I don't mean that Craig doesn't love his kids; he does, a lot. He's a real good father. But they're like anchors pulling him down. And Michelle used them every chance she got. He felt guilty all the time."

She looked directly at me, lifting her head. "When we first started going to bed, Craig was like a different man. He had something good to look forward to, not just one day of dahlias after another. You saw him in the shop; even his attitude toward customers was different."

I tried to think back to before Alison came, but I couldn't remember how Craig had behaved then.

"We really had to be careful. Henderson is such a small town. If word ever got out, it would have been disastrous for the business. And, of course, everyone would have blamed me."

She dropped the sheet and leaned forward in her chair. I could tell that it was a relief for her to have someone to tell this to. I might not be the one she would have chosen for a listener, but since I knew anyway . . .

"It doesn't matter to the good folks of Henderson that Michelle was a bitch most of the time, that she squandered the money Craig worked day and night to make. She didn't sleep with other men, she just sashayed around in her designer jeans and handknit sweaters. She just teased. But that was okay here in Henderson. It was okay that Craig was miserable. It was not okay that being with me made him happy, and made me happy too. No. You know what people would say?"

"What?"

"That I stole him, like he was one of Michelle's sweaters. I stole him away from her."

"Why didn't he divorce her?"

Alison sighed. I could see that this was not a new subject for her. "The children. They're Catholic. Michelle would have raised hell in court. She'd have called him immoral, a bad influence on the children. He'd have gotten to see them once every other weekend at best. He couldn't live with that. He really cares a lot about those kids." She sat back with a thud. "And he also didn't want to leave them to be brought up by her."

There were questions I could have asked, but Alison had told me all about their relationship which could reflect on Michelle's murder and the Bohemian Connection. There was still one dangling end, however. "What about those two guys we met on the beach today? What possessed you to accept their offer?"

Alison gave her head a sharp shake, flinging her hair back. It caught momentarily behind her ears then fell loose. "You mean, didn't I know they assumed we were hookers? Of course I did. I was just pissed off about Craig and his willingness to sweep me aside while he panders to his guilt. I wanted to get at him, but I could hardly do that, not the day after his wife died. But then these guys came along. I knew what they were after and I thought, why not?"

I said nothing.

"I didn't go to bed with them, if that's what you're thinking. I just drank their liquor. It appealed to me to make use of them. I told them I'd meet them at their motel tonight. That appealed to me, too. I suppose they're still waiting." For the first time, she smiled. "Stay out of motels tonight, Vejay. I told them I'd bring you along—for an extra hundred."

Now I was making enemies of people I didn't even know.

"Do you want a glass of wine? There's still half a bottle left." She pulled open the refrigerator door, extricated the bottle, and got two glasses out of the cabinet. With the refrigerator on it was no wonder there was noticeable electric usage here.

I said, "You're more careless than the Bohemian Connection. Didn't Ross teach you the method?"

She brought the wineglasses back to the table. "Actually he did. It was one of the things he bragged about. And Craig and I did bring our own sheets and pillows. I don't think the old lady will ever guess anyone's been in her bed."

"Ross was still the Connection when he lived with you, wasn't he?"

"Yes."

"How did he handle that while he was living in San Francisco? I thought the Connection needed to be here and on call."

"Most of the time it wasn't necessary for him to be here. It's only a big thing around Bohemian Week. Ross was here then. He'd been here the year before. He popped back occasionally for a day. And he could always be reached through his father. His father resented his having moved away. He never really acknowledged that Ross was living in the city, not working for the realty company, but he did know where he was."

"So clients called Ross in the city?"

"No. The local suppliers left messages with Ross's father telling Ross to get in touch with them. The outside people didn't know Ross wasn't living in Henderson. They had the phone number they'd always used; they called, Ross wasn't in; they left messages; Ross called back. For them nothing had changed."

"But Ross wasn't here for the entirety of Bohemian Week that year, was he?"

"No. I told you that."

"He never planned to be, did he?"

"Maybe not. He told me he was just coming for the weekend."

I could feel my excitement rising. "So Ross wasn't going to work as the Bohemian Connection that year, was he?"

"I guess not. He didn't mention it, and I wasn't thinking about it, so I didn't ask."

"Didn't he have some records, papers, addresses,

directions? He couldn't have kept everything in his head."

"I told you, Vejay, what he had in my house was just clothes and a couple of magazines—nothing was written in them. He had less than a bagful of stuff and none of it was worth anything. Believe me. I was pretty mad at him. If he'd had anything worth money I would have sold it."

"Didn't he mention any records?"

She sipped the wine. "You're right—he did. He said once that it was a pain keeping track of some of his suppliers. They kept moving around. And it's not like they were listed in the Yellow Pages. So he needed to keep a record of how they could be contacted—where they were, or through whom they could be reached."

"Were there other records?"

She lifted the wineglass again, thinking—or pretending to think. She seemed to want company regardless of the subject that company discussed. "I think he mentioned other notes or records but I can't remember specifically. It was a long time ago."

I took a breath and said, "It was eight years ago, wasn't it?"

"Could be."

"Michelle wanted to go to the Bohemian Ball but she wasn't quite eighteen. She'd be twenty-five now. That's eight years."

She nodded.

"Ross never left you except for the Sunday afternoon when he went to see his family, right?"

"Yes."

"Did he talk about the Bohemian Connection with anyone when you were together?"

"No. I never heard him mention it to anyone but me the whole time I knew him. He had some sense."

Gravel crunched outside.

"The driveway! The sheriff?" She jumped up. "The shop truck's out there!" She grabbed the sheets, bottle, and her glass, and ran for the door.

Flicking off the light, I followed.

By the time I shut the door, Alison had run around the far side of the house and disappeared. I raced back into the cemetery. In the darkness, I stumbled over a low gravestone and sprawled onto the leaf-strewn path. Pushing myself up, I raced toward my blanket and supplies, grabbed them, and ran for the parking area.

Headlights flashed on me. I turned toward Maria Keneally's driveway. I couldn't make out the vehicle for the glare of the lights, but I could see that it was cutting across the pine needles of the yard toward the cemetery path—toward me.

I ran for my truck and jumped in. The headlights were coming from the graveyard now, thirty yards behind me. The vehicle was picking up speed. I started my engine and spun the truck toward the road. The truck bounced as I gunned it over the potholed road, through the old cement pillars, and onto Cemetery Road. The lights were closer behind me, reflecting glaringly in my eyes.

I stepped on the gas, taking the sharp curves on Cemetery Road much too fast, barely missing barreling into the hillside, then, in reaction, swerving too wide the other way. The passenger-side wheels skidded over the edge of the road. The truck leaned over a steep drop to the river. I jerked the wheel back just in time for the tires to grab the pavement.

The headlights were closer now. I turned right

onto Zeus Lane, barreling down the incline. North Bank Road was ahead. On it, cars moved cautiously. A Volkswagen crossed the intersection. I stepped on the gas, yanked the wheel right, and cut in behind it, barely missing the fender of a Cadillac. Its horn blew.

Once in traffic I looked in the rearview mirror to get a glimpse of Zeus Lane. But the vehicle that had tailed me was not visible. There were no headlights and no flashing lights.

With a sigh, I decided it was not the sheriff following me.

But my relief was short-lived. If it wasn't the sheriff, there was only one other possibility.

I didn't take time to consider my pursuer's plans, and I was not about to give him a chance to demonstrate. Spending the night at home was out. For a single woman with no luggage, checking into a motel this weekend would be a big mistake. It was Vida's house or nothing.

I didn't expect her to be pleased to see me. But I hadn't counted on waking her up either. Eyes half shut, she opened the door, pointed me to one of the boys' empty rooms, and stumbled back to bed.

Vida may have needed sleep, but clearly not as much as I did. When I woke it was to the smell of linguisa frying. Slipping into my jeans and T-shirt, I hurried to the kitchen.

There was no dining room in Vida's house, but the big paneled kitchen made up for that. With leaves in it, the table would accommodate ten. Now there were only four chairs around it. And there was ample space to work at the counters or walk to the refrigerator. It was a kitchen for a family of cooks.

Sun flowed in through the windows and the glass door. The fog had burned off early and the day would be hot. Vida was already dressed for it in jeans and a yellow gingham halter.

"Should I ask what brings you here?" she said, turning from the stove. From her tone it was clear that she hadn't forgotten our last conversation, and her exasperation with me.

"Someone was following me. I almost drove off Cemetery Road."

Another person might have said, "So you decided to lead them to my house?" but Vida just looked worried for me. "Oh, Vejay," she said, "are you okay?"

"I'm fine. I lost them in town, but I thought going home was tempting fate."

"You did the right thing. Here, let me get you some coffee. It's brewed." She moved from stove to counter to fridge, seemingly intent on the job of coffee pouring. When she handed me my cup, she said, "You think this is connected to Michelle's death, don't you?"

I nodded, then took a cup of coffee. It was strong and hot. It made me realize anew how hot it was in the house. The sun was clear; there was no suggestion of cloud or remnant of morning fog. I glanced at my watch. "Ten o'clock! I didn't realize it was that late. What time is Congressman Tisson speaking?"

Vida gave a tight shrug, her back to me. She didn't want to talk to him; she didn't want me to. But that couldn't be helped. I hurried into her living room to find the paper. It took me a couple of minutes to come up with the article and discover that the ceremonies started downtown at eleven.

"Vida," I said, back in the kitchen, "I have to see him. I have to tell him about Michelle's larvae. Michelle would have wanted that."

"Michelle's dead." She was still facing the stove, but her shoulders were hunched in anger.

"I'm on the right track, Vida. If I weren't I

wouldn't have been followed last night. Whoever followed me wasn't kidding; he wasn't lagging behind, keeping an eye on me; he was forcing me to go down that hill at sixty miles an hour."

"Maybe you ought to be glad you're not injured . . . or dead."

"I am. Michelle wasn't so fortunate."

Vida looked stunned. Then with the concentration she had given the coffee pouring, she spooned mushrooms and black olives into the eggs. Her shoulders remained hunched tight around her neck.

"Vida, let me tell you what I discovered last night before you say you'll be satisfied to let things lie."

With exaggerated care, she stirred the egg mixture and scooped it onto plates. Then she added the linguisa.

When we were seated at the table, I said, "Ross brought Alison up here the weekend of the Bohemian Ball. That was eight years ago. Do you remember what also happened that weekend?"

She put two pieces of sourdough bread in the toaster. "No."

"Mr. Remson, Ross's father, had a heart attack and died."

Slowly, she said, "You're right. I'd forgotten that was the same weekend."

"Before then Ross had been the Bohemian Connection—"

"Vejay, I don't want—"

"You said you'd listen."

She gave a grudging nod.

"Ross had been the Bohemian Connection before that. Alison said he had done it the year before and could be contacted in San Francisco if there was anything he needed to do in the off-season. And he popped up here occasionally."

"Yes, that's true. I remember we'd see him walking down North Bank Road and assume he was back, and then discover he had just come back for a couple of hours."

"So he wasn't going to be the Connection that summer. He must have decided to cut his last tie here, and move on permanently. Alison told me he had friends in San Francisco he needed to get away from—dangerous friends." I took a bit of eggs. "Good," I murmured. "That weekend had to be the weekend that Ross was going to pass on the Connection job to his successor, and disappear into the back country, or up north, or wherever."

"How do you know he'd go to that trouble? Ross would be more likely to just leave. He wasn't famed for his responsibility."

"The Bohemian Connection meant money. It's unlikely he was just giving it away. He may have been selling it, or he may have been planning to pass it on to someone who would send him a share of the profits. He would need the money while he hid out. The thing is, that weekend he and Alison were here. Michelle and Craig, and Ward and Jenny: they were all here. Ross was with Alison all weekend and never mentioned the Connection. The only time he was alone was when he went to see his father. So he must have planned to pass on the Connection there. Whatever records he kept were not in San Francisco. The only other place they could have been was in his father's house. So he must have planned to meet his successor there and give him the records."

Vida stared, her fork held halfway between her plate and mouth. "My god! That *would* be enough to give old man Remson a heart attack. He never conceded that Ross was the Connection. Everyone in town knew it, but old man Remson couldn't accept anything bad about his son. But to see Ross admitting it . . . To know what Ross had been and what that had been doing to his business . . . He cared almost as much for that business as he did for Ross. I can see him having a heart attack."

I took a sip of coffee. "When a man has a heart attack, there's a lot of commotion. There's panic; there's rushing around. The ambulance is called. Maybe the sheriff comes. Did Ross care at all about his father?"

Vida put down her fork. "Ross didn't have much feeling for anyone, but he wasn't totally insensitive. He wouldn't just go on with his business transactions while his father lay dying at his feet."

"Then picture the scene. Old man Remson is digging the hole for the new cesspool. Ross and the person who he chose to succeed him are standing nearby. Ross is holding the records, probably in a metal box or two. If they're too bulky to hold he has them next to him. And then the old man crumbles. Everything's in a flurry. Ross is caught up in it. Any of the others—Michelle, Craig, and certainly Ward and Jenny—would be too. The neighbors rush over. The ambulance comes. Ross doesn't know whether the sheriff will come by or what will happen. He doesn't want to leave the records in the house. If the old man dies, Jenny may go through the house and find them. He can't give them to his successor because there are too many people around to have someone carting boxes down the stairs unnoticed. He's already got the money. And what he wants is to leave right away. The last thing he can deal with

is to be caught up in the business of going to the
hospital and staying in town until his father recovers
or dies. Ambulance runs are reported in the newspaper—in the Fire Report. If Ross's pursuers checked,
they'd know exactly where to find him.

"So Ross wants to get out. He's not the Connection anymore. The records are no longer vital to
him. The new Connection will have some problems
without them but he'll have to get by on what Ross
told him. Once he's contacted a couple of sources
they'll pass the word to the others. What's important is to get the records out of sight. So where does
Ross put them?"

Vida said nothing.

"A cesspool should last thirty years. It shouldn't
be forcing the liquid into the leach lines after eight
years—not unless there's a blockage."

CHAPTER
19

It was already eleven o'clock as we came down the stairs, me hurrying, Vida lagging behind.

"Come on," I said. "This isn't Congressman Tisson's only stop today. We don't want to miss him."

"Vejay, I still don't know about this. Craig wouldn't want a congressman involved in Michelle's death."

"He would want Congressman Tisson to get that cesspool opened if he thought it would lead to Michelle's killer. You all want that, don't you?"

Vida sighed. "We do and we don't. But I don't see what dredging up Bohemian Connection notes from eight years ago is going to tell us about Michelle's murderer."

"Maybe nothing. But there could be a note, a letter, something indicating Ross's successor. If Ross's records are in a strong box they'll be as fresh as the day they were dropped there."

By unspoken agreement we passed up both trucks and headed for North Bank Road on foot.

The traffic was worse than any day so far this summer. Horns honked; drivers stuck their heads out their windows, craning necks to spot the reason for the holdup. As we crossed at Zeus Lane, I said to Vida, "I wouldn't have thought Congressman Tisson was this popular."

She smiled. "He's not. And he'll be even less pop-

ular when all these people discover he's the reason
they're stuck in traffic."

"But if he's not that big a draw, why would they
hold him responsible?"

"Just look."

We had made our way behind the shops and were
going down the slope to the town beach. It took me
a moment to realize what Vida was indicating.
There were no cars parked on the beach! The entire
beach parking area, from the concession stand
where I had gotten my parking ticket yesterday to
the line of shops that backed onto the slope we were
descending, had been roped off and was filled with
people sitting on blankets with their picnic coolers
or standing in small groups, drink cans or ice cream
cones in hand.

"That must be seventy-five parking spots gone.
No wonder no one can find a place to park. No
wonder all those drivers are sitting on North Bank
Road with their engines idling. Everyone in town
must be on the beach. I've never seen this place so
packed."

Vida almost laughed. "They're not here out of
civic responsibility. They're here to see what Tisson
will do."

I recalled David Sugarbaker telling me about a
congressman who'd come to Henderson some years
back and been given a hard time. He'd said Michelle
had laughed when she'd described that incident.
"What do you mean, Vida, 'What he'll do?' "

"The congressional district covers four counties,
so a little town like Henderson is hardly a priority. If
there weren't all the newsmen here this weekend
because of the Bohemians, you can bet Tisson
wouldn't have bothered to come. We don't see these

guys often. The last one was here four years ago. And he did the same dumb thing as Tisson—took over the beach, cleared the parking lot, and caused a colossal traffic jam. When the drivers figured out why they were sitting there, they slammed out of their cars and trucks—just left them on North Bank Road—and stormed down to the beach, raising hell. They actually put some burning paper under the podium."

"I heard they burned it down."

"The story has grown over the years. I'll bet most people here heard what you did. Unfortunately, Tisson wasn't one of them or he wouldn't have made the same mistake. But that was years ago—different congressman, different party, different advance men."

We made our way through the narrow path left by two blankets. On them, coolers were open and beer cans were being passed around.

"The last congressman," Vida said, "was an hour late. People were pretty tanked up by then."

I glanced at the podium. "Well, Tisson's already here. What do you mean about the crowd being here to see what he'll do?"

"They're expecting, or at least hoping for the same reaction from the drivers. Some of the local guys who know about the last incident will be caught in the traffic. You can bet they'll lead the onslaught."

"But Tisson's pretty good at dealing with hecklers. He had a lot of chances when he was campaigning."

"Good entertainment for all," Vida said, looking out over the crowd. Her tired face showed a mixture

of sadness and reproach. Fleetingly, I wondered if
her sons were in the crowd.

The dignitaries stand had been set up behind the
concession stand. On it were four chairs. It was
draped with the standard red, white, and blue crepe
paper.

Grabbing Vida by the hand, I squeezed between
onlookers, stepped over coolers, and around small
children. As I moved toward Tisson, I recalled Michelle's comment to Sugarbaker—after dealing with
the crowd Tisson would be glad to turn his attention
to something so inoffensive as her mosquito larvae.

Congressman Tisson, a short man with thinning
red hair, sat in one of the middle chairs facing the
speaker, our mayor. But his attention was clearly
elsewhere. I wondered if he had heard anything
about the possibility of a disruption. But surely if
he'd heard of his predecessor's mistake he wouldn't
have repeated it. In front of the stand were two sheriff's deputies. I glanced around for Wescott, but he
wasn't visible.

Michelle had planned to make the most of this
moment. Following Michelle's lead, I said to Vida,
"Let's catch Tisson before he starts speaking."

"Vejay, he's got plenty to think about now without you—"

Ignoring that, I pushed forward, pulling Vida
along. The area in front of the stand was filled with
reporters and television cameras from the networks
and national papers as well as the local papers. They
would provide much better coverage than Congressman Tisson's speeches normally received. The newspeople had come for the opening of Bohemian
Week. Those who remained were here in hopes of
something breaking—a policy statement by one of

the politicos, or better yet a scandal. They were waiting. I wondered how many of them knew about Tisson's predecessor's debacle.

To my right a contingent of bathers, still holding towels and ice cream cones, had pushed in close. But the north side was relatively clear. I headed there. If I could get to Tisson, trade a warning of his upcoming danger for his help in opening the cesspool . . . Was that what Michelle had had in mind?

Despite the loudspeaker system, the mayor's words were muffled. They seemed to be dropping into the sand.

I was halfway around the back of the stand when a deputy grabbed my arm. "Hey, lady, you can't go there."

"I have to talk to the congressman."

"You can't do that now."

"It's important."

"Doesn't matter. No one can disturb him."

It was Michelle's complaint; I'd give her style a try. "He's a public representative and I am one of his constituents and he needs to hear what I have to say."

"Not now, lady."

"He'll be sorry if he doesn't."

"Is that a threat?"

"No, of course not. It's just—"

"Then it'll have to keep."

I glanced up at the podium. Congressman Tisson was still seated. To the deputy, I said, "It'll only take a minute. It has to do with . . ." I considered trying to explain what was awaiting Tisson, but rejected that and said, "With a murder."

He hesitated, assessing me, then looked at the

congressman. Finally, he said, "I can't take that responsibility. I'll have to check . . ."

The rest of his sentence was smothered by applause. The congressman walked to the front of the stand. The deputy turned around briefly to watch, then, facing me, he shrugged.

"That's okay, Jeff," Vida said to him.

"My god, you know him?" I said.

"Of course," she whispered. "He was in school with my oldest boy."

"Then you talk to him. Tell him how important this is."

"I still don't see why we have to do this."

The crowd applauded. Whistles of approval came from the rear.

"Because," I said to Vida, "the killer knows those records are there. The killer knows I'm looking for him. If we don't get those records now, they'll be gone."

"He's not going to dig them up today, Vejay."

"Maybe not, but he tried to intimidate me last night. If he suspects that I've told you what I know, you won't be safe either."

Suddenly my words seemed very loud. Congressman Tisson had stopped talking; the crowd was silent. I wondered if he had paused for applause and found none forthcoming.

On North Bank Road horns honked.

As one the audience turned toward the street.

I moved closer to the podium. Had I allowed myself to be put off too long? Had I missed the moment when I could have had some leverage with him?

Tisson started speaking again, but his tempo was off.

The crowd was still facing the street.

Tisson's voice wavered; his gaze followed theirs.

The horns stopped. From the street came metallic clunks—doors slamming? Then six men, beer cans in hands, stormed down the slope, yelling, "Clear it out, clear it out!" I assumed they were referring to the beach.

Tisson looked baffled; the crowd amused.

Groups—men and women—came down the slope from both ends of the beach. The chants degenerated into hoots and catcalls. Congressman Tisson raised his voice, but the hoots got louder. The deputy sheriff was using his walkie-talkie to call for reinforcements. The television cameras swung around. Reporters readied their microphones as the protesters moved toward the platform.

The mayor moved to the front of the stand. Taking the microphone from Tisson's hand, he called for quiet.

But the noise increased.

"Please folks, let me . . ."

The hoots grew louder.

"Folks, listen . . ."

They didn't. The mayor's words only fueled their protest. Some raised beer cans as they yelled, others clapped rhythmically. The seated audience joined in with glee. For three or four minutes the mayor tried to regain control.

"In Henderson," Vida said, "you don't keep a man from driving his truck and get away with it." Even she was smiling. Only Congressman Tisson and the mayor looked disturbed.

The deputy moved in front of the stand.

Had Michelle foreseen all this? Was this the moment she planned to approach Tisson? Maybe. It was the last chance I would get. In another minute or two he'd either gain control of the crowd or he'd decide there was no point in staying and giving the television crews more footage of his humiliation. I walked quickly around back. "Congressman Tisson," I called.

He didn't move.

"Congressman Tisson!"

He glanced around.

"Congressman Tisson, you can help one of your constituents—right now. You can help with a big problem."

He looked at the crowd in disgust, then back to me.

I stepped on a support beam and hoisted myself onto the stand. "It has to do with finding a murderer."

His brow wrinkled. I recalled his reputation for quick saves.

At the front of the stand, the mayor was still trying to quiet the crowd.

Feeling a pang of guilt about Vida's plea for no more publicity, I shifted closer to Tisson. I knew what he'd do with the tale of Michelle's complaint. "I'm asking your help for a local woman, a twenty-five-year-old mother of two, who lived here in town. She was murdered this weekend. You were her representative. She planned to ask your help. She was murdered before she could do that."

Tisson glanced at the mayor, then at the crowd, assessing them, and back to me. When he nodded, I could tell he'd made his decision. "What did she want to ask me?"

The crowd was quieter. Quickly I explained about Michelle's death and her attempts to get action on her mosquito larvae and her neighbor's cesspool.

When I finished he asked, "What was her name?"

"Michelle Davidson."

The crowd was almost silent now. Congressman Tisson strode forward and took the microphone with an air of one who, rather than having caused the commotion, has been called in to rescue the day. "Ladies and Gentlemen, I just heard that one of your neighbors, right here in Henderson, was killed Thursday night. A young mother with two small children. Her body was tossed, like garbage, into a sewer construction hole."

I turned away from where Vida was standing. I didn't want to see her reaction to this.

"And the thing Michelle Davidson was going to do, ladies and gentlemen, was to ask my help in dealing with a bureaucracy. You've all had problems with bureaucracies, haven't you?"

Where there had been screams of protest minutes ago, now there were wary nods of agreement. I could see where Tisson got his reputation for thinking on his feet.

"Like poor Michelle Davidson, you've followed the rules and the bureaucrats have ignored you. Am I right?"

"Right!" someone yelled.

"Michelle Davidson made a complaint to the Environmental Health Department once a month, every month since last Christmas, and still, in July, nothing has been done. Nothing. I say that is too long!"

"Right!" The response came from voices on both sides of the crowd.

"It's six months too long!"

"Right!"

"I say, the time to have action is now! Right now!"

The crowd broke into applause. The cameras were all on Tisson now. He turned to me at the back of the stand. "Who owns the cesspool?"

"Ward McElvey."

"Is he here?"

I hesitated, not wanting to be so visible on the stand. The congressman pulled me forward. "Look for him," he demanded.

It didn't take long. "He's over there, in the blue shirt and slacks."

"Ward McElvey, come on up here. We can handle this right away. Come right on up."

Ward looked around furtively, as if considering the possibility of escape, then shrugged and stepped forward and up onto the stand. As he moved to the microphone, Ward glared at me, then shook his head to flick his hair in place, and smiled tentatively at Tisson.

"I'm sure, Mr. McElvey, that you are as saddened as everyone in town is at Michelle Davidson's death."

Ward nodded.

No wonder Vida hadn't wanted to mention Michelle's death to the congressman. Even I hadn't expected him to play it for this maudlin a show.

The crowd was silent. Tisson asked Ward about the mosquito larvae, then poked the microphone toward him. "Why haven't you cleared up your cesspool problems, Mr. McElvey?" he demanded.

Ward took hold of the microphone gingerly, then moved it close to his mouth. "I've been waiting to see if I'll hook onto the sewer or have to get a new cesspool." He spoke fast, nervously, into the too-close mike, so that his words melted into the electronic rumble. I doubted anyone ten feet away could understand him. "Everyone in town has debated whether or not to hook on. It's not cheap, you know." Sweat covered Ward's forehead. His skin was as red as Alison's bikini.

"Another bureaucracy, the sewer bureaucracy, folks, that's what we have here. One bureaucracy failed to act, and another kept neighbors from working out their problems together."

The crowd murmured approval.

"But now, Mr. McElvey, as one of the leading citizens of Henderson, as a neighbor and friend, I'm sure you want to grant Michelle Davidson's last request and dig up that cesspool. I'm sure you want to leave her family in peace."

There was no sound. Tisson looked at Ward. Ward looked at the crowd. Tisson reached for the microphone he'd given Ward, but Ward kept hold.

"No," he said.

"What?"

"No, I'm not going to dig up my cesspool. I told Michelle—"

The crowd shouted him down.

"Mr. McElvey, surely you can put aside personal concerns when your neighbor, your next-door neighbor, has been killed." Tisson had taken the microphone. Now he held it out to Ward, but Ward didn't take it.

"No!" He turned and jumped down from the stand.

Tisson stared after him a moment, then said into the microphone, "Is there a judge here?" He turned to the mayor. "Didn't you tell me Judge Watson would be here?"

"He was supposed to be. Probably caught in traffic."

"Judge Watson?" Congressman Tisson called.

People in the crowd looked around, but no judge appeared.

"Ladies and gentlemen, I am not going to be stopped. Michelle Davidson's last request will not be ignored. Sheriff! Let me see the sheriff."

From the edge of the crowd, Wescott made his way toward the stand. I sat down on one of the chairs.

"Sheriff," Tisson said into the microphone, "I need your help in finding Judge Watson. He's on his way here. He should be here any moment. He's just caught in that traffic jam."

"Then he won't get here till tomorrow!" someone yelled.

I looked at the crowd to see their reaction, but there was none. They had forgotten that Tisson was the cause of the traffic. They were with him in his quest.

"What kind of car does the judge drive?" Tisson demanded of the crowd.

"Buick," a man yelled. "Maroon Buick. New."

"Thank you. And thank you, Sheriff."

Wescott hadn't said a word.

It took only a few minutes for Wescott to discover which way Judge Watson would be coming and to send the deputy I had talked to along North Bank Road toward Santa Rosa to bring him here.

Ward McElvey was nowhere in sight now. Briefly I considered rushing to his house, but no matter what he did not want discovered, he couldn't dig up a well-buried cesspool in an hour.

The crowd had doubled now. The beach was

jammed. Craig and Alison stood, not right together, but not far apart, near the south end of the beach. I spotted Jenny making her way down the slope. Someone must have told her something was going on; maybe they even knew her own husband was the villain of the drama. In the middle of the crowd, I noticed Father Calloway. And with a quick glance, I checked that Vida was still where I had left her.

"Judge Watson, right up here," Congressman Tisson called. "Make way, folks. Let the judge through."

When the judge, a tall, thin, bald man of about sixty, arrived at the stand, Congressman Tisson reviewed Michelle's death and her complaint in loving detail. He had the crowd with him; they nodded in response to every phrase he uttered. They murmured approval as he asked the judge to issue an order on the spot to dig up that cesspool "and even in death give Michelle Davidson justice!"

The judge assessed the political situation as quickly as had Tisson, and making a statement about the responsibility of the judiciary to the people, he ordered the cesspool opened.

"And now, folks, who will volunteer to dig? Which of you strong men?"

He didn't need to ask twice. Enough men to excavate North Bank Road approached the stand. And then, with Tisson and the news crews in the lead, the entire crowd headed toward Ward McElvey's cesspool.

I found myself in the middle of the crowd. It was an odd mix of people. As the marchers hurried along, propelled by the anticipation of a show and the chance of being seen on the evening news, they fell into two groups: the locals who knew Michelle and were sad, angry, or still surprised by her death; and the tourists to whom Michelle was just another body waiting to be buried. To them, her death—in a sewer—was cause for bewilderment, or for laughter.

We poured onto North Bank Road, blocking both lanes of traffic and filling sidewalks on both sides. There must have been three or four hundred people, and like any procession, we were picking up people as we went.

As we passed Davidson's Plants and started up Zeus Lane, a hand touched my shoulder. David Sugarbaker. "What is this?" he asked. He looked alert, his sandy curly hair shiny clean. Tan arms and legs extended from a T-shirt and shorts. "Someone said they're going to dig up that cesspool I was checking." He stared down at me in confusion and fear, as if the dig would be an indictment of his own work.

"Didn't you hear Congressman Tisson's speech?"

"No. I just came into town. I was going to get some breakfast. There's this place that advertises a champagne brunch on Sundays."

"Well, what led to this dig is a long story."

"Tell me. We've got time. A cesspool isn't six or eight inches under ground, you know. And that soil will be hard. It would never have passed the perk test. It'll be murder to shovel up. You've got plenty of time to tell me the whole tale."

"Okay," I said. The crowd was thinning a bit as we moved up the steep street. Those unused to climbing in the midday heat were falling back, the rest of us pushing ahead. Away from the river now, any suggestion of cool was gone; the sun glared down on the macadam; the heat seemed to foam up to surround us. Wiping the sweat off my forehead, I told Sugarbaker about Ross Remson having been the Bohemian Connection, about his flamboyant activities when he lived in Henderson, and then his move away. "He lived in San Francisco then, but he came back for Bohemian Week."

"When he made most of his money?"

"Right. That's how it was until eight years ago. By then he was gone for all but that week. Michelle had married her husband. Ross was living in San Francisco with Alison. But he had to get out of San Francisco, away from his dangerous associates there. So the first weekend of Bohemian Week Ross brought Alison here. He had all his records here. Michelle and Craig, his closest Henderson friends, were in town. His sister Jenny and her husband, the one who owns the cesspool, were here. Alison says Ross left her and went to his family's house. When he got there his father was digging the hole for the cesspool."

"Geez. That's a big job for one man, particularly an old man."

"It was. He had a heart attack. The ambulance came. And Jenny told me that when she looked for Ross to drive her to the hospital, he had gone. The flurry of the ambulance arriving would have covered his escape."

"What about his records? Did he take them with him?"

"I doubt it." I recounted my reasoning to him. "So I've been assuming that the records are in the cesspool—"

"And they're forcing the liquid into the leach lines!" Sugarbaker looked delighted, as if the whole Remson family crisis had been arranged to solve his leach line problem.

We turned onto Half Hill Road. The pace slowed. I looked up at Sugarbaker. He kept nodding as he considered the cesspool blockage.

I quickened my pace, moving to the front of the line. For once I was thankful for my winter of climbing steep wooden stairways and clambering up muddy driveways. Sugarbaker, with his long legs, had no trouble keeping up. The congressman was breathing heavily. The judge's face was red. Sheriff Wescott strode beside them. And directly behind were four men with shovels they had managed to acquire one way or another as they walked. The reporters hovered, sweating, but never falling back. Most of them crowded around the congressman, but several talked to the men with shovels. Forming a wider circle around the group were the cameramen, walking crablike, looking up from their lenses only to wipe the sweat from their foreheads.

There was a brief pause by the sewer construction hole. Cameras panned from it to Michelle's house to Ward's and back to Congressman Tisson. Then the group made their way around the hole and up Michelle's stairs to the deck.

The congressman looked around expectantly. "Okay, men, dig it up."

No one moved.

Tisson stared at the shovelers.

One said, "You got to tell us where it is first."

Tisson looked puzzled. As a former city-dweller, I knew what he was thinking—the cesspool should be under the toilet. He would have no idea that that needn't be the case. Cesspools were where the hole could be dug and the line connected. Many people who hadn't dug the holes themselves had no idea where their cesspools where. We meter readers, who faced the danger of falling into abandoned cesspools after the lids rotted away, knew the above-ground signs. I started to move forward, but Sugarbaker beat me to it.

Before I had taken a step, he was next to the congressman, introducing himself, and explaining that he'd been here investigating the complaint. It was clear from Tisson's expression that the last thing he wanted was evidence that the bureaucracy had moved on Michelle's complaint without his prodding. Stepping between Sugarbaker and the cameras, he instructed him to lead the men to the hole.

It was between the houses, partway up the incline, no more than ten feet from Michelle's garage and the mosquito larvae.

The crowd filled Ward and Jenny's stairs, spilled over onto their yard, stamping for footholds on the steep ground. They covered Craig's yard, using the seedlings for handholds. And they filled the street, pushing so close to the sewer construction hole that the sheriff's deputies had to move them back. Men lined up by the diggers, ready to relieve them.

But Sugarbaker had been wrong about the soil. It wasn't hard. And he had been wrong about the box. It wasn't yards deep. The crowd was still arriving when the diggers struck the top of the redwood cesspool box.

The sheriff stepped forward. "Okay, hold it there." He took a shovel and began to pry the top loose.

I leaned over the railing and looked down. The box was less than four yards away.

The sheriff lifted the lid.

The smell was awful.

It took only six shovels full of excrement to uncover what was inside. The sheriff ordered the diggers to step back and called for a garden hose. He aimed the water into the box. The diggers vacillated between moving forward for a glimpse inside the box and jumping back to avoid the ricocheting spray. I leaned over the railing.

The sheriff turned off the hose nozzle. The water stopped.

Inside the cesspool were the remains of a body—very decomposed.

I swallowed hard.

Grimacing, the sheriff leaned close to the skull. When he stood up he shook his head and said to one of the deputies, "There's a gap between the front teeth."

The onlookers seemed to gasp as one. The sheriff stood motionless, looking down at the decomposed body of Ross Remson.

Thirty seconds passed, then it was as if the still picture came to life. The cameramen pressed in. Congressman Tisson began speaking. Reporters crowded around. And the news of what was in the cesspool passed in a visible wave through the crowd.

I moved back to the far side of Michelle's deck, staring blankly at the crowd. David Sugarbaker came up beside me.

"I can't get anything from those guys," he moaned, pointing to Tisson and his entourage. "What does all this mean?"

"It means that Michelle Davidson was murdered to stop her from complaining about her mosquito larvae—to keep the cesspool from being dug up."

"Then her death had nothing to do with this Bohemian Connection you were telling me about? That Bohemian Connection job wasn't passed on that weekend?"

"No. The Bohemian Connection job did pass on, but not as Ross intended. But that's not why he was killed."

"Well, why was he killed? And who is the Bohemian Connection now?"

I thought a moment, letting my eyes survey the

crowd. I couldn't find the familiar faces now, not Jenny, or Ward, or Craig or Alison, or even Vida. The crowd had pressed forward, leaving Mr. Bobbs standing a few feet off from its outer edge.

Turning back to Sugarbaker, I said, "The question that has bothered me all along is why was Michelle's body put in a place where it was bound to be found no later than Monday morning. All along I've looked at it as if the killer had to put it down there Thursday night to get rid of it then. Like the Follow-up I told you about. But I'd forgotten that there's another end to Follow-up—that's when the folder comes back. And that was the reason Michelle's body was dropped into the sewer hole. It wasn't only because the killer couldn't dispose of it Thursday night. It was so the killer *could* deal with it at a convenient time before Monday morning. Like Mr. Bobbs said about Follow-up—the idea is to deal with it at a time when you can give it your best attention. That's what the killer planned. The killer didn't expect me to find it Friday. It was reasonable to assume that it would still be there Sunday night."

"But who?"

"There was one person who needed to put off disposing of the body till then. And there was only one person who could have taken over the job without Ross's approval."

"Listen, could you—"

I looked over the crowd again. The killer was gone. But I knew where the killer would go.

Suddenly the crowd was quiet. A reporter's voice rang out. "Congressman Tisson, how does this connect with this woman's complaint?"

"Well, that's hardly an issue now," the congressman said.

"Hardly an issue!" Sugarbaker fumed. He looked toward me and back to Tisson.

"Go on," I said, giving him a push.

He leapt forward.

Momentarily I was tempted to follow, to tell the sheriff what I had figured out. But he was right in the middle of the crowd. It would take a good ten minutes just to elbow my way to him and then who knew how long to get his attention and to convince him who the killer was. Suppose he wouldn't believe me—again. I wasn't about to give him that opportunity.

I started up the hillside, making my way across the path behind Ward's house, through the crowd and up the incline from there, the way Sugarbaker had gotten back to his car Friday afternoon. My boots slipped. I grabbed at branches, pulling myself up, scraping for handholds in the earth until I could reach another branch and clamber on up. When I got to Cemetery Road, I turned left, hurrying on, thinking of the killer and of Michelle Davidson's incredible bad luck.

I hadn't had to guess how the killer knew I would be at Maria Keneally's house last night—following me from my own driveway was easy. But I had wondered why, why then? Now I realized that it was to keep me from seeing Congressman Tisson. I had stood in front of Michelle's house yesterday afternoon telling Vida that I intended to pass on Michelle's complaint to Tisson. I had argued with her that it was vital. Michelle had been killed to prevent her from asking him to push her complaint about the cesspool, and thus, to keep Ross's body from being discovered. Poor Michelle had stumbled inno-

cently upon the one cause that would prove fatal to
her.

Cemetery Road was empty now. Everyone was
either downtown or in Ward's yard. I hurried on
past the dead-end roads, along the turn to the cemetery, then through the old cement pillars.

The average person wouldn't have thought that a
simple talk with a congressman would lead to his
insisting on opening the cesspool. I had caught Congressman Tisson at an advantageous moment. The
killer had no reason to assume Michelle would have
made use of that same opportunity. The only way
the killer would have suspected how much a congressman could do would be if he had heard David
Sugarbaker talking about the Environmental Health
Department and how the employees jump when a
congressman calls.

The cemetery was deserted, too. In the evening
shade the tombstones blended with the dusk. But
now, in contrast to the splotches of bright sun, they
seemed more sepulchral. I hurried past them, glancing at the Maria Keneally marker.

The house of the living Maria Keneally looked
empty. But I knew the killer would be there. The
house was the logical hideout—the only place isolated enough for use by the Bohemian Connection
and still within walking, or running, distance from
town. I wished it were night now, when the darkness
would protect me, when a light in the house would
tell me if anyone were there. As I neared it, I realized
that I was the only one who had made the connections that pointed to the killer. The killer would
know that too. My investigating had hardly been a
secret. And the other thing that I recognized, and

hoped the killer wouldn't, was that no one knew either of us was here.

The back door was closed, the screen pulled shut. I circled around the side, staying close to the bushes, with each step placing my foot slowly, carefully, noiselessly down, avoiding the leaves and branches on the ground. The bedroom windows were closed, the broken bathroom window just as it had been yesterday. But the killer wouldn't have had to use that way in. If there was one thing the Bohemian Connection would have, it would be a good set of skeleton keys. And I wouldn't have to use the bathroom window either.

Keeping low under the windows, I made my way around to the garage. The door inside, from the garage to the living room, didn't lock. Maria Keneally had complained about that. She'd complained but she hadn't been about to spend the money to have it fixed. After all, she'd told me, the garage door locked. That would keep anyone out. And for most prospective intruders it would. But Maria Keneally's meter was in her garage. I was her meter reader. And I knew where the key to the garage was.

I unlocked the door, and opening it inch by inch to avoid its squeak, I let myself into the garage. I walked carefully across the garage, skirting boxes and ladders, an old broken television; years of accumulated excess. It looked like Maria Keneally kept everything she owned in the garage—everything except her antique pistol. Why couldn't that be here too?

But it was in the living room, right inside the garage door, in the end table drawer, right where Maria Keneally could grab it and face off any local ne'er-do-well who tried to break into her house.

At the door to the house I stopped, listened. There was no sound from inside. Was the killer in the bedroom, at the other side of the house? Could I slip into the living room, grab the pistol from the end table drawer . . . ?

I turned the handle, pressing it down to keep it from squeaking. I pushed the door open half an inch at a time. Only the near slice of the room was visible —a worn armchair and a lamp. I pushed the door further. The front door came into view and beside it a coatrack with Maria Keneally's winter coat hanging from it.

The door flew open. A hand grabbed for my hair and yanked me off balance to the floor.

"Gotcha!" Jenny shouted. She picked up a pistol from the end table behind her. It was old, heavy— Maria Keneally's pistol.

I inched back on the floor.

"Don't try to get away now," Jenny said, laughing. "I'm very good with a gun. Shooting was the one thing Ross did teach me."

The shades were up, but curtains covered the windows. Even with the bright sunshine outside, the room was dark. On the far side of the front door was the dining area. Jenny had already made herself at home there. She had pushed the table to the wall. A backpack with a roll of sketch paper sticking out sat atop it. And an end table lamp sat on the table. This would be where she planned to do her sketching.

"This is all you could bring here without your car, isn't it?" I said.

"Ward's car!"

"Ward's car," I repeated. "It wasn't a useful car for you." I thought of the big windows of the Pacer.

They were part of the reason Jenny had dumped Michelle's body in the sewer construction hole. The Pacer was hardly a car you could leave a body in. And the sewer hole had blocked the McElveys' driveway. Jenny couldn't even have put the body in the car and then the car in the garage. And with Ward's guests, the Underwoods, already in the house expecting to be fed and entertained all weekend, Jenny couldn't drive off long enough to safely get rid of Michelle's body that night without arousing suspicion. So the body went into the sewer hole, on Follow-up, to be taken out Sunday night after the Underwoods had left.

"You really planned ahead, Jenny. You checked this out for the Bohemian Connection work, didn't you? That's how you found the pistol, isn't it?"

She smiled.

"Ross wasn't planning to give you the Connection job, was he?"

She smiled again, this time glancing down at the gun. "No. Ross wasn't about to give me anything. Ross didn't give; he only took—not even took, he grabbed. He was my father's *son*. He never had to stay in the house with my mother when she was too crazy to be left alone. He raced around on his motorcycle; he went to dances. I was the one who had to watch her when she went manic. I had to make sure she didn't get out where people might see her. I had to guard the phone. I had to drop everything. I couldn't paint; I couldn't read; I couldn't even go to the bathroom. It would have looked bad if people had seen how crazy she was; it would have damaged the business. People don't want to buy a house from a crazy woman's husband. That's what Daddy told me.

"I never had friends; I couldn't. I couldn't stay after school to do anything. I could never invite anyone over. No one would have wanted to come in there anyway. No one would have liked to see her pacing around inside. I had to watch her. But she did escape once. And you know what happened?" Jenny stared at me with a smile, an angry smile, an expression out of sync with itself.

"She drowned, didn't she?"

"Yes, yes. I let her out and she drowned." She stared first at the gun and then at me, still with that disparate expression.

I could imagine the mix of relief and guilt she had felt then, but I didn't want to ask about that. I didn't want to do anything that would drive her deeper into her emotional turmoil. Once she was submerged in that, any chance of my reasoning with her would be gone. In this secluded house, she could shoot me without anyone hearing. She could stick my body in the garage next to the broken television.

Still, I had to know about the murders. Watching her reaction, I said, "Tell me how you killed Ross."

"I liked killing Ross." Her smile was paper-thin. Her fingers tightened on the pistol. "Daddy loved Ross, only Ross. Ross was his *son*. He always forgave Ross. He left Ross the house, did you know that? *My* house. And the business, the business that Ward made work. Do you know what Ross planned to do?"

"When?"

"After my father died, of course. Ross watched him die. He watched him dig the hole. Then he watched him fall. He watched as the ambulance took him away. Then do you know what he said?"

"No."

"He said, 'Well, the old man's dead. This shack is mine. The bourgeois business is mine. I'm going to unload them both before he's in the ground and never see this town again.' That's what he planned to do, sell my house, sell the only business that would give Ward steady work. We would have had no place to live, nothing to live on. I worked for that house. I watched that crazy woman all those years while he rode around on his motorcycle. He was going to sell my house; he was going to sell the business, to make me go to work all day, five days a week." Her fingers were white against the gun. "I would never have been able to paint."

"So you killed him?"

She flashed that smile again, like a paper floating over a fire. "It was easy. He didn't expect it. I hit him with a pipe, just like Michelle. You don't have to hit them as hard as you'd think. You don't have to kill them that way. You just have to stun them and drop the body into the slime. The slime does the rest. It was so easy. So nice. So appropriate. It was so good, so right to see Ross dead. Even Daddy would have agreed."

She continued to smile, more concretely now, as if the recitation of facts was pulling her back toward reality. "There was dirt piled right beside the cesspool hole, just waiting. I didn't shovel much in over him. Just enough to cover him. Then I drove to the hospital. If Ross had taken me to the hospital, I wouldn't have had to drive alone. I wouldn't have killed him, you see. But he wasn't going to."

"What happened to his Bohemian Connection records? Did you just leave them in the house?"

"Yes. There was no need to do anything else with them."

"And then you became the Bohemian Connection?"

Jenny laughed. "Ross would have been so angry. He was going to have an auction for the job. That's why he came home. He was going to call some of his suppliers and have them come over and bid for the job. But he didn't get the chance. I killed him first." She laughed again. "Sometimes I wish he hadn't died, so he could see me. He would be so furious. He thought he was keeping everything so secret, like he was this big important man with his clandestine job. But I always knew where he kept things. When I was in the house, watching that crazy woman, I'd take out his boxes and go through his records."

"And the people he dealt with, did they think he had passed the job on to you?"

"They didn't care. They knew me. They trusted me as much as they trusted Ross, maybe more. By that time I knew more about the area than he did. They'd seen me with him. The local people knew we didn't get along, but the out-of-towners didn't. They just knew I was his sister. If they called the Bohemian Connection's number, I answered."

The whole operation was becoming clear. She was right; it was so simple. "So the men who needed to contact you came up to you on the sidewalk and had their pictures sketched, right?" How many times had I seen an unlikely subject in Jenny's chair? How often had I noticed a man handing her *a* bill, a bill for an eight-dollar sketch, and getting no change?

"It wasn't just for the money." Jenny stared at me, a pleading look in her eyes. "I did like taking Ross's job. I did need the money. Ward never could keep his mind on the little matters of business that make the money to live on. With him it was always

Sunset Villas, or high-rises, or pie-in-the-sky things. We could never have lived on his commission from selling houses. But that wasn't the real reason. Those men I met, they were important. Sooner or later one of them would be an artist, or a gallery owner, or a critic, and he would see my work, and he would appreciate it like no one in this little town does, and then he would arrange for me to show it in a city, where an artist should be. You see that, don't you?"

"You did all this for your art."

She smiled. She looked down at the gun, then at my face again. Her finger arched on the trigger. She lowered the barrel toward my heart.

"Jenny," I said, trying to keep my voice even, "you promised to sketch me, remember?"

"No, you just wanted to nose around." She straightened her arm, moving the gun closer to me.

"But I wanted your drawing, too. Don't you remember I told you I'd looked at artists doing drawings of people when I was a kid. But I was too young then. I didn't have the money for a drawing—not a good drawing—not one by an artist with talent."

Her eyes narrowed. I tried to tell from her expression how much touch with reality she still had. Would my reasoning make any difference? Or had the thrill of death become too strong?

"It'll only take a few minutes," I said.

She glanced from my face to the sketch pad.

"You've got your sketch pad. Your charcoal is here. Mine is the only face you'll have to sketch as long as you stay here."

Jenny laughed. "I can draw you day after day. I've never done a dead person. I've never drawn a corpse as it decays, as the skin droops in around the bones. You have good bones."

I swallowed hard. "Corpses smell, Jenny."

"I'm an artist. A real artist suffers for her art." Her eyes looked at once blurry and piercing, as if they had honed in on some private truth, leaving reality behind. She was as crazy as her mother.

"And there are holes in the cemetery," she said. "When they dig a hole the earth is soft. I can add another corpse. I like holes."

The cemetery was full. But I didn't want to keep Jenny concentrating on methods of my disposal. I needed her diverted, not thinking of me. I said, "Did you like putting Michelle in the sewer hole?

"I had to. There was no place else. It was Ward's fault. Like everything." With her free hand she extricated a piece of charcoal from the pack, keeping her eyes and her gun on me. "He invited those people, those Underwoods, for the weekend. He didn't ask me if it was convenient. My busiest week, and he invites strangers, and then expects me to entertain them, to be there listening to their bourgeois talk, to cook for them. I had to make dinner. I had to sit and watch their bland faces as they talked, and listen to Ward go on and on about floor plans and unit sizes and access and variances. I thought I couldn't stand another word. But then they went to bed. They were old. They didn't stay up late. I left. I had to get out of the house." She glanced from me to the backpack on the table. "Take the pack off the table. Hold it arm's-length in front of you. . . . Okay, now put it on the floor. Take the sketch paper out. There's a portable easel in there. Take it out. You can set it up. That's it, just snap the support in place. Now put it on the table. Okay. Back up, back to the wall."

I moved against the wall, pushing the backpack to one side. "So you went outside," I prompted.

"Michelle was at the bottom of the stairs. She'd been drinking. I could tell. You could always tell with her. Drink makes some people happy like Daddy, but not Michelle. It made her a bitch. She was real angry. Her face was pointed, like a weasel or a fox. It was all sharp edges of flesh, not bones. She said, 'That house should have been mine, mine and Ross's. If you, all of you, hadn't bugged him, he wouldn't have left here. You think you can have it your way, Jenny,' that's what she said, 'you think you can have it your way; well, you can't. That cesspool, you think you can go on letting that leak into my garage, don't you? Well, you can't.' She said she was going to talk to the congressman. She told me he had a lot of power, that he would make them dig up the cesspool. She told me the man who came out to check the mosquito larvae told her that."

Jenny moved the easel closer and glanced quickly from me to it and back to me. "I said I didn't believe her. But she told me the man from Environmental Health came out and told her exactly what to do."

"So you decided to kill her?"

"I had to, you see." She drew a circular line on the pad.

"You hit her on the head, right? Then you dropped her body in the sewer hole. You couldn't put her body in the car where it would be visible to anyone who walked by. You couldn't drive it an hour into the woods when you had company who would wonder where you'd been."

Jenny looked angrily at me. "I couldn't even put the car in the garage because the damn sewer hole blocked the driveway." She smiled. "It was fitting, don't you think: I couldn't use the garage because Michelle fussed about the sewer construction, so I used the sewer for her body."

I caught my toe on the edge of the backpack. "So you planned to take Michelle's body out of the sewer hole in the middle of the night Sunday and put it in Craig's nursery truck when you drove to the flower market in San Francisco?"

She added another line to the sketch.

I edged the pack closer.

"I could have left the body anywhere. I planned to drop it in Golden Gate Park in San Francisco. They have plenty of bodies there. Then I could have gone on to the flower market. If I left here half an hour early I wouldn't even have been late. I still could have gotten the alstroemerias Craig wanted." She glanced back at the sketch pad.

I inched the pack closer. It was almost within reaching distance. "What will you do now?" I asked.

"I know people, people in the hills. I have connections. Hey, hold still. Push that backpack this way, slowly."

I leaned forward slowly. I grabbed the pack and flung it at her. The gun fired. I rolled under the table. The easel crashed down. The gun fired again. I could feel the breeze of the bullet passing my ear. I leapt forward, grabbed Jenny's foot, and yanked her to the floor. She smashed the gun into my shoulder. My hand went numb. I grabbed her arm with my other hand. The gun fired wide. I swung my arm at her neck. It was enough to stun her.

The rest of Sunday was consumed with the aftermath of Jenny's arrest: the statement for the Sheriff's Department (given to a deputy while Wescott questioned Jenny) and the avoidance of the reporters who were thronged outside. I was afraid my house might be surrounded by reporters, too, but it was clear of them. After I saw the news coverage, I understood why. I had gotten off unscathed with regard to publicity. Congressman Tisson hadn't mentioned my role in encouraging him to push Michelle's complaint, and the Sheriff's Department wasn't going out of its way to say a civilian was involved in the killer's arrest. For me, that was just fine; the fewer people who knew, the better, particularly if one of the ignorant was Mr. Bobbs. (I didn't want him connecting my uncharacteristic visit to the office on Saturday with the murder investigation.)

Michelle's funeral was held Tuesday. The entire town trekked to St. Agnes' Roman Catholic Church, filling the little church, the parking lot, and trampling the beds in which Father Calloway had never been able to grow vegetables. For the local papers the story was the high point of the year. Reporters and photographers from San Francisco, Sacramento, and Los Angeles, still in town for Bohemian Week, zeroed in on the funeral. Crews from three television stations covered it. They described Michelle as a heroine, a martyr for morality, family, and decent living. They called her a crusader.

It was an embarrassment of riches for them, this unexpected story with its divergent ramifications. Some reporters emphasized the murders of "high school sweethearts" in prose worthy of gothic romance, others concentrated on Congressman Tisson's insistence on opening the cesspool. Some focused on the issues of prostitution and power concentrated in the Russian River area that week. A befuddled Mrs. O'Leary of the anti-hookers' group was interviewed three times. And none of the reporters could resist the illegal and immoral acts of the Bohemian Connection. It was a muckraker's paradise.

"If only Michelle could have seen this," more than a few people on my route said. "She would have been in seventh heaven." Some voices trailed off awkwardly here. Others plowed on to give their own analyses of the events. With every homeowner anxious to discuss the situation with whomever appeared at his door, it took me two hours longer than usual to finish my route.

Wednesday, in reaction to the previous days' overload, no one mentioned Michelle or her murder. Perhaps there was nothing more to say.

It wasn't till that afternoon that I got back to the sheriff's department to read over my statement. This time I was ushered into Sheriff Wescott's cubicle. From behind his government blue desk, he motioned me to a blue chair. In back of him was his overloaded bookcase. A pile of paper-filled boxes I recalled from my visit here several months ago suggested that he was either a very busy or very inefficient man. His desk was nearly invisible under memos, reports, and notices. His expression, as he looked at me, had the same ambivalence as Jenny McElvey's, if not the intensity.

To break the silence, I said, "I was surprised at how little people were hurt by the coverage of Michelle's murder."

Wescott leaned back in his chair. "The papers and television, you mean? They could have done a number on some of these folks. Look at Ward McElvey, for instance. You'd think the husband and the brother-in-law of two Bohemian Connections would be damned by the publicity. But every news report I've seen has pictured him as a decent, hard-working Joe, putting himself out to support his crazy in-laws. He's come out of it looking like a prince."

I nodded. "Even Jenny will get something of what she wants—someone to support her and time to paint."

Wescott nodded, but he wasn't smiling now. "And that nerd Sugarbaker, look at him. Is there any mention of him bar-hopping in the county car, on a weekend, yet? None. If you believe the papers, he's a dedicated public servant investigating cesspools on his own time."

In spite of Wescott's glower, I couldn't help laughing. The front page photo in Monday's paper showed David Sugarbaker pointing to the cesspool while an obviously disgruntled Congressman Tisson looked on.

But Wescott didn't share my amusement. He continued to glower.

"And you," I said, "you didn't come out of this too badly, either. You've been quoted all over the place. You got the killer the same day as the cesspool was opened. That's not bad publicity for a sheriff, is it?" When he didn't answer, I goaded, "Is it?"

He leaned forward, elbows on the desk. "Well, okay, it could have been worse. But that doesn't excuse the fact of your crossing our cordons, or putting me in a position where I had to drag an innocent citizen out of a bar. If word of that had gotten out I could have been—"

"But it didn't. And you—"

"It doesn't excuse your breaking into a house with a felon hiding in the living room."

"Look, you've already given me a ticket."

His mouth wavered, then he laughed. "I guess another warning to stay out of trouble isn't going to do much good. But, you know, Vejay, one of these days you're going to break the law and not get off with just a slap on the wrist."

"I suppose now you're going to tell me to stay out of bars—at least with you."

There was the slightest pause before he said, "I'll have to trust your judgment on that one." He glanced down at a report on his desk and then back at me. "How's your boss taking all this?"

"Mr. Bobbs? He doesn't know I'm involved. But he actually did act on my Follow-up suggestion—the one asking for two-way radios in the PG and E trucks."

"What did he decide?"

"He said he gave it his best attention and then routed it to Joan Theadorams, who's in charge of the agenda for the budget committee."

"And what did she do?"

"She put it in *her* Follow-up!"